THE ORPHAN'S OATH

Victorian Romance

FAYE GODWIN

Copyright © 2025 by Faye Godwin

All rights reserved.

No part of this book may be reproduced in any form or by any electronic or mechanical means, including information storage and retrieval systems, without written permission from the author, except for the use of brief quotations in a book review.

PERSONAL WORD FROM THE AUTHOR

DEAREST READERS,

I'm so delighted that you have chosen one of my books to read. I am proud to be a part of the team of writers at Tica House Publishing. Our goal is to inspire, entertain, and give you many hours of reading pleasure. Your kind words and loving readership are deeply appreciated.

I would like to personally invite you to sign up for updates and to become part of our **Exclusive Reader Club**—it's completely Free to Join! I'd love to welcome you!

Much love,

Faye Godwin

FAYE GODWIN

CLICK HERE to Join our Reader's Club and to Receive Tica House Updates!

https://victorian.subscribemenow.com/

CONTENTS

Personal Word From The Author — i

PART I
Chapter 1 — 7
Chapter 2 — 14
Chapter 3 — 28
Chapter 4 — 40

PART II
Chapter 5 — 49
Chapter 6 — 62
Chapter 7 — 71
Chapter 8 — 85

PART III
Chapter 9 — 99
Chapter 10 — 125
Chapter 11 — 158
Chapter 12 — 164

Continue Reading... — 170
Thanks For Reading — 173

More Faye Godwin Victorian Romances! — 175
About the Author — 177

PART I

CHAPTER 1

Ellie's world ended the day her mother's heart stopped beating. Tears fell from her eyes as she looked down at her mother's lifeless body lying on the narrow cot. Her father died the day before, and now Ellie was alone in the world. The thought terrified her. When her parents fell ill of influenza, Ellie had done a great deal of growing up to take care of them, but at twelve years of age, she was still a child.

She stayed with her mother as long as she could, until there was a knock on the door. "It's time to come out, child," said the soft male voice. "It's done."

Ellie left the room to find three men looking soberly at her. She avoided the eyes of her landlord, who looked at her with impatient indifference, and instead looked at the vicar and the parish constable. When she spoke, her voice shook. "My parents both have– had– penny policies. It should be enough to bury 'em." At least they wouldn't be subjected to a pauper's grave.

The vicar nodded. "The arrangements will be made. I hope you understand that this will have to be a private affair due to the nature of their deaths. You will be the only mourner."

Ellie nodded. Even though she understood the words he was saying, it was difficult to think about anything except the grief consuming her.

The landlord snapped his fingers in front of her face to get her attention. "Do you have a way to pay the rent, girl?"

Her bottom lip trembled. "No, sir," she whispered.

"Speak up!"

But she couldn't. She knew she would start crying if she even tried. Instead, she shook her head.

The man scoffed in disgust. "Then I expect you to be out of here by the end of the week. As soon as the funeral is done, you must be gone, and do not try to take any possessions with you. They will be used to settle your debt."

"Y-Yes, sir," she stammered, feeling a sinking feeling in her stomach. Stark fear broke through the excruciating anguish she was feeling about the loss of her family.

The penny policies kept her parents out of pauper graves, but the funeral service was sparse. They were buried in plain, wooden coffins with only herself and the vicar present.

When the funeral service was finished, Ellie stayed at her parents' graves and allowed herself to weep openly. What she wouldn't give to feel her mother's hug or hear her father's laugh one more time. They never had a comfortable life, but at least Ellie knew she had been loved.

She walked home to find the locks had been changed during the funeral, meaning she was officially homeless on the streets of London. Not knowing what else to do, she started to walk aimlessly down the sidewalk. She felt numb. All her emotions were cried out over her parents' graves and despite not knowing where she would sleep or get her next meal, she didn't feel fear, or much of anything at all.

Night fell and the weather proved to be cold and damp. Ellie shivered and wrapped her arms around herself as she turned down an alleyway. Maybe she could find a quiet place to curl up and fall asleep.

The alley was dark and quiet, sandwiched between a tavern and a hotel. Faint laughter and music could be heard from either side, which made Ellie's heart ache.

She walked down the alley and looked for the darkest corner to hide away for the night. However, when she reached a shadowy corner, a weak cough told her she wasn't alone.

She froze. "Who's there?" she whispered.

Someone whimpered– a child.

"It's all right," Ellie said, taking a step forward. "I won't hurt ya."

She heard shuffling sounds before a small face appeared. The little girl could be no older than six. She had a gaunt face and wide, blue eyes. She stared at Ellie with a slightly fearful expression on her face.

The twelve-year-old managed a smile. "Hey there. My name is Ellie. What's yer name?"

"Ida," the girl said, her voice scratchy. "We didn't mean to cause no trouble."

"There's someone else with ya?" Ellie peered behind her.

Another figure came out of the shadows. This girl was even younger than the first one. She was a few inches shorter, and her face was slightly plumper, but it was clear the two of them were sisters. The younger girl gave Ellie a hesitant smile.

"What's yer name, little one?"

"Daisy, ma'am."

Ellie couldn't help but smile. "There ain't no need to call me ma'am." For the first time in weeks, she felt a small spark of humour. The feeling warmed her heart. "Are you two alone?"

Both girls lowered their eyes. "Our parents done left us," Ida said softly. "They said they couldn't feed us, so they left us in the road one day and..." Her bottom lip trembled as she fell silent.

Ellie's heart went out to the poor girls. As awful as it was to have her parents die, at least she knew she had never been abandoned, at least not by choice. "I'm by meself too," she said. "Me parents died." She drew in a shaky breath. "But maybe the three of us can stick together. It's better than being alone, ain't it?"

The two girls nodded and smiled shyly at her.

Something warm, almost like happiness, settled deep in Ellie's chest. For the first time since her parents died, she felt like she had a purpose again, and that purpose was taking care of these two girls. "Let's find somethin' to eat."

"We don't got no money," Daisy said hesitantly.

"I know. Me, neither." However, her stomach rumbled. The only thing she had eaten that day was a bowl of weak broth and a crust of stale bread. It was clear the two sisters had eaten less than she had that today. She didn't like the thought of stealing, but she couldn't let these little girls starve either.

Trying to hide the conflict and guilt she was feeling, Ellie managed a smile. "We'll just make do. Come on. There's a market not too far from here." She held out her hands and the two girls grabbed them with obvious relief.

Because it was a Saturday, the local market was bustling with activity. Women carrying shopping baskets strode from stall to stall, buying produce, bread, and other provisions. The three girls went unnoticed as the crowd moved around them, intent on haggling for the best prices from the sellers.

Ellie felt unsure, and a little scared. She had never stolen before, but these two girls were counting on her. Frustration rose inside her. What was she doing? She couldn't help these girls. She didn't know how to help herself. All she was going to do was get them caught and beaten by an angry seller. As she looked around, she met the eyes of a boy. His clothes were slightly ragged, like hers, but his posture was confident and relaxed. His brown eyes sparkled with mischief as he smiled at her.

Very pointedly, he approached a baker selling loaves of bread right next to the three girls. The baker was already being swarmed by people trying to buy his goods.

Without blinking or even slowing his pace, the boy grabbed a loaf of bread from the corner of the stall and tossed it to Ellie. She grabbed it, hardly daring to believe what had happened. She turned to look for the boy, to thank him, or ask him why he would help them, but he had already disappeared into the crowd.

Ida tugged on her hand and pointed to the edge of the market. "This way."

Ellie and Daisy hurried after Ida to an abandoned market stall next to a public house. All three of them hid under the stall together. The three of them were sheltered from most of the wind here, and they would be spared if it rained. Ellie broke the loaf of bread into three pieces, making sure she took the smallest piece for herself. The three of them scarfed down their portions ravenously before huddling up together to sleep.

Elli closed her eyes. Her stomach wasn't full, and a chill had crept into her bones. Her heart ached over the loss of her parents. But her stomach no longer ached ravenously, and Daisy and Ida warmed her up enough, even on the hard ground. She managed to drift into a semi-peaceful sleep.

CHAPTER 2

THE NEXT MORNING, the three girls woke up just after sunrise. The market was mostly empty except for a few stalls open to sell for an early-bird crowd that had risen with the birds. Daisy smiled and hugged Ellie. "Good mornin'."

Ellie smiled. "Good mornin' to you, too."

Ida stared off into the distance, a pensive look on her face. "Where do we go now?"

Ellie didn't have an answer for her. Where could they go? She knew from talking to the girls the night before that none of them had been on the streets for long, and they didn't know how to beg or steal. Perhaps there was a workhouse willing to take them in, but the thought made her shiver with trepidation. Yet how long could the three of them realistically survive on the streets?

Before she could come up with an answer, a hulking shadow passed over the market stall and Ellie looked up to see a large man glaring down at them.

"Get outta here, you mangy rats," he growled at them. "I ain't got no coin or food for you, and I have wares to sell. Out before I call the constable."

Fear sliced through Ellie as the three of them scrambled to their feet. Ellie scooped Daisy up in her arms and grabbed Ida's hand as they ran away from the market. The three of them didn't stop running until they were alone in an alleyway. All of them stopped, bending over to catch their breath.

However, the three of them didn't have long to recover before several pairs of footsteps approached them. Ellie looked up to see three boys now surrounding them, their sneers twisting their faces. Ida hid behind Ellie's skirt.

"What do we got here?" one of them said. "Three little mice, lost in the streets."

The other two guffawed.

"Please," Ellie said. "Let us go. We don't got nothin' for ya."

"Ya got yer clothes, don't ya? And yer shoes. Those must be worth something to the rag seller." The leader took a step forward, towering over Ellie. "Ya can give them to us now, or we can take them off yer dead bodies."

Before Ellie could react, someone appeared behind the leader and pressed a knife against his neck. She recognized him as the boy from the day before and relief spread through her.

Her saviour wasn't looking at her. All his attention was focused on the street boy he was holding at knifepoint. The other two boys tensed up, ready to strike, but he spoke calmly and with a deadly edge. "One wrong move and yer friend here is dead."

The two of them froze.

He pressed the knifepoint deeper into the boy's neck. "The three of you can leave with yer lives intact or with slit throats. I know none of ya have knives, but I assure you, I'm very quick with mine."

The gang leader muttered something under his breath.

"What was that?" her saviour asked.

"Okay!" the street boy choked out.

He lowered the knife and shoved the boy away with one smooth motion, putting himself in between the street boys and the girls. "I don't want to see ya three again."

The three boys scampered off, and the remaining one turned to the girls with a grin as he pocketed his knife. "Hello again, you three. The name's Luke Cooper."

"I'm Daisy," shouted the little girl with a grin. "Thank you, mister."

Luke grinned down at her. "It's nice to meet ya, Miss Daisy." He shed off his tattered jacket and handed it to her. "Here. Ya can use this more than me."

Daisy smiled and wrapped the jacket around her thin shoulders.

Ida hid behind Ellie's skirts, still looking a little nervous. Ellie smiled at the older boy. "You've helped us twice. I don't got nothin' to repay ya with."

His smile was warm and sent strange butterflies through Ellie's stomach. "Whatcha need to repay me for? I'm happy to help three ladies like yerselves."

Daisy giggled. "Ladies? Us?"

Luke grinned down at her. "The three of you are as pretty as ladies. As pretty as princesses."

The absurdity of it made the little girl giggle. Ellie couldn't help but smile at the sound. She never expected to be happy again after her parents died, but these two little girls, and Luke, were doing the impossible for her.

Luke's eyes flick back to Ellie's face. "The three of ya must be new to the streets."

She nodded, not sure about what else to say. She didn't feel quite comfortable telling him their full stories. At least, not yet.

"That's all right. Stick with me, and you'll be fine," he said, grinning. "It ain't so hard. I've been living here for years, and I got it all sorted."

Ellie nodded. "Thank you. But... why?" She couldn't help but ask. "Why 'elp us at all?"

His brow furrowed for a moment, as if he never considered that question at all. "Because I want to," he says. "Plain and simple. Better than being alone, ain't it?"

Ellie had to agree with that. She would much rather be with her three new friends instead of being alone. "Thank you. For everything."

"Don't need to thank me," he said. "Now, let's get goin'. I'm gonna show you a whole new side of London."

The three girls followed Luke through London as he showed them the best spots for begging.

"Beggin' is safer than stealin'," he said as they reached a busy part of the city next to a church. "Folks are a lot less likely to call the coppers when they give their food and money willingly instead of you takin' it by force. You just gotta be careful to not get nabbed in the process, an' stay away from constables. I'm not so good at beggin' now that I'm fifteen. But the three of you will be brilliant at it." He grins. "Come on, let's give it a try."

Luke faded into the background as the three girls stood on the street corner, feeling uncertain. Ellie remembered seeing beggars on the streets before, but she never paid them any mind, so she wasn't sure how to do it herself. Ida and Daisy were even less sure than she was.

She looked back at Luke, who nodded encouragingly at her. Feeling a little more assured, Ellie took a deep breath and stuck out her hand. "Please, sir," she said to the nearest gentlemen. "Spare a coin?" The man looked at her with disgust before carrying on down the road, but Ellie was undeterred. She simply turned to the next person.

Daisy watched her with wide eyes before following suit. She took a couple of steps forward. "Please, ma'am," she said to a woman. "Could ya spare something?"

After a moment of watching them, Ida joined in, sticking a trembling hand out as she shyly asked a stranger for a coin.

The minutes stretched by without much of anything until a man threw a couple of farthings at Daisy's feet as he passed. Daisy scooped them up quickly and waved, grinning, at the departing man. "Thank ya, sir! 'Ave a good day!"

A heavy hand touched Ellie's shoulder, and she gasped and turned around, fearful until she saw Luke's face. "We 'ave to go," he said. "Constable."

She didn't bother to look around for the strange man. She didn't want to know what would happen to her if a constable really did catch her. Instead, she grabbed Ida's hand as Luke scooped Daisy up into his arms. They ran away until they were far away from the danger.

Luke started to laugh when they were safe. "A 'ole 'alf penny, Daisy! Good work!"

The little girl beamed up at him, clearly already taken with him.

But Ellie felt a little uneasy about something he said when he was teaching them how to beg. "Did ya help us because you need little girls to beg for ya?"

He looked at her with a trace of hurt in his eyes but not surprise. "It's true I can't beg so well anymore. Nobody cares to give coin nor work to a fifteen-year-old vagrant, but I can get by on me own just fine. I meant what I said about not wanting to be alone no more. I can protect you lot easy enough, and three girls on the streets need protectin'. There's a lot of good-for-nothin's who will do 'orrible things to ya, and I don't like that thought one bit."

Ellie bit her lip. She wanted to believe him. It would be nice to trust this strange boy to protect her. But she had Ida and Daisy to think of as well. She needed to be careful to keep them out of a bad situation. "'Ow do we know yer not going to do 'orrible things to us?"

No trace of his usual good humour could be seen now. He stepped forward, and Ellie braced herself for him to shout at her or slap her. Daisy and Ida both looked between the two of them, nervous looks on their faces.

However, when he spoke, his voice was soft. "I swear never to 'urt ya, Ellie. Or Ida, or Daisy. And if ye ever think I'm mistreatin' ya, or takin' more than my fair share, then ya can leave me behind. I won' come after ya, I promise."

His words and expression were so sincere, that Ellie couldn't help but believe him, even though it felt natural to be suspicious of random kindness from strangers. How often were people who were not her parents, kind to her in the past? She nodded. "I believe ya."

He smiled again, all his good humour coming back. "Jolly good! Now follow me, I know a few other places perfect for begging."

Luke showed them around part of London, telling them the best places to beg, and how to score the most sympathy. Daisy was a natural at it, with her big, pleading eyes, and innocent, grateful smile. By the end of the day, they managed to scrape together enough money for some stale, leftover bread from the baker. Luke made sure to take the smallest portion. Ellie looked at him, surprised. "Don't ya want more?" she asked. "Yer the biggest of us all."

He shook his head. "All I did was keep look out for the constable," he said. "I meant it when I said I would only take my fair share."

Ellie smiled at him gratefully. "Sorry I got so 'spicious of ya earlier. Ya haven't done nothin' wrong."

He gives her a small, crooked smile. "Don' blame ya for it. It's smart to be on yer guard, 'specially on the streets."

Ida yawned. "I'm sleepy, now that I'm full. Can we find 'nother market stall?"

"Not a good idea," Luke said. "Vendors can be territorial over their stalls. Best to find a place that nobody cares about."

"I think I saw something like that," Ellie said hesitantly. "A couple of streets back."

Luke grins at her. "Lead the way."

She took them down a street full of crumbling buildings, on the bad side of town. There was an uneasy feeling in the air, as if danger was lurking around every corner, but no one was around; at least, no one they could see with the sun setting and the fog rolling in. She stopped in front of the most dilapidated building of them all, an old bakery. The walls were crumbling, and the front door was hanging half off its hinges. It was clear no one had used this bakery in years.

"This will do," Luke said. "At least for the night. We can't be actin' all fussy when night is rolling in."

All of them went through the front door. Even inside, they could feel the force of the wind through the cracks in the building. Ellie could dimly see the splintering floorboards, littered with rubbish, old rags, and a thick layer of dust. The thought of sleeping in such a place made her feel colder than the wind ever could.

Luke walked through the place, to behind what used to be the counter where baked goods were displayed. A large grin lit up his face as he looked down at his feet. "You struck gold, Ellie! If my feelin' is right, you found us a cozy li'le home."

She frowned. "How do you mean?"

"Come 'ere."

The three girls scampered to Luke's side as he knelt next to a trap door. He opened it up to show a rickety ladder leading down to a basement. "No wind down 'ere," he said, climbing down the ladder. His feet hit the dusty floor with a light thump. "It's dry, too. Only a bit musty." He looked up. "Come on, then. If the ladder can 'old me, it'll certainly 'old you lot."

Daisy went down the ladder next, then Ida. Luke helped them off the ladder by picking them up gently and setting them on the floor. Next, it was Ellie's turn. She carefully climbed down the ladder, and when it was her turn, Luke held out his hand to help her. She took his hand, which was a lot warmer than her own. She loved the feeling of it. It comforted her somehow. She felt a blush rise to her cheeks and was grateful for the very dim light, which would keep him from seeing it.

Once she was safely on the ground, she looked around. She could barely see anything. The air was stale and musty, but it was warmer than upstairs, simply because the wind didn't reach this low.

"We'll be able to get a proper look at the place in the morning," Luke said. "For now, let's huddle up and get some sleep."

They didn't move too far from the basement entrance because they didn't know what could be lurking in the shadows. Luke lay on the ground, using his arm as a pillow. Ida and Daisy curled up against him and hugged each other as they used Luke's jacket like a partial blanket. They both fell asleep immediately. Ellie hesitated and sat down a short distance away.

Luke gave her a curious glance. "It's going to be a mighty cold night for you all the way over there," he said.

"I..." she blushed, knowing he was right. Luke was taller than them, by a lot. Even though he was skinny, his body would radiate body heat, at least compared to her wind-chilled body. She didn't think twice about cuddling up with Ida and Daisy the night before. But it felt different with Luke. "I'm not sleepy yet," she said instead.

He raised an eyebrow skeptically, but didn't accuse her of lying. "I'm not either," he said. "Today was too exciting. I'm not sleepy at all."

"Exciting?"

"Of course. I made some new friends. Friends are always good on the street." He grinned.

"What were you doing before you found us?"

He shrugged one shoulder, careful not to disturb the girls. "This and that. Begging and stealing mostly and running from the coppers. Sometimes I'd get lucky and get a bit of honest work for a couple of farthings, or a scrap of bread. But not often. An' at night, I'd catch some sleep when I needed to, or when I was pretty sure I wouldn't be caught."

"You didn't have any other friends?"

A shadow passed over his face. "Not a lot of friendly folks on the streets. I fell in with some boys a few years back, but I left them behind a while ago. They started takin' boys and puttin' them on ships for forced labour. I won't do that, no matter how hungry I get. Stealin' some bread or meat is one thing. Grabbin' people and makin' them work on ships is another." In the near darkness, a muscle twitched in his jaw. "I planned to just get by on me own, but that's awfully lonely after a while. Then I see three girls in the market who clearly don' know the first thing about stealin' or livin' on the streets, an' I know I can help." His expression brightened with a smile. "What 'appened with you three, anyway? You 'aven't been 'omeless for very long."

Ellie shook her head. Her heart twisted as she thought about her parents. They only died mere weeks ago, but it felt like another lifetime. "My parents…" she took a deep breath as she felt an intense lump in her throat. She thought she had cried out all her tears at the graveyard, but talking about them brought a fresh wave of grief.

Luke's eyes softened. "Oh, you poor thing," he whispered. He reached his hand out and grabbed her own. She squeezed his hand, focusing on Luke's warmth and strength.

Ellie wiped her eyes. "Sorry," she said. "There's no use cryin'."

"Cry all you want. I won't 'old it against ya."

She hugged her knees to her chest and sobbed. She missed her parents so much and even though she was so grateful for Luke, Daisy, and Ida, she was scared. "They got ill," she finally said as her tears lessened. "I didn't 'ave no money for the landlord when they died, so here I am."

He was silent for a moment before he spoke. "What's it like, 'aving parents?"

She looked up at him, surprised. "You never knew yers?"

He shook his head. "Never knew me dad. Mum died when I was barely three. I don' remember her, not really. Sometimes I think I can picture her face, but not much else."

"What did you do?" she asked in amazement.

He smiled, but there was no humour in it. "I begged, of course. I was small enough to hide from the coppers easy enough. Sometimes, good folk would take pity on me and give me some food or even an old blanket. Sometimes, I would fall in with other street urchins an' give 'em my begging money for protection. I made do."

"That's awful," she whispers.

"It don' matter. I was luckier than a bunch of folks. I'm still livin', ain't I?" He shifted slightly to prop his head up on his fist. "So, what's it like to 'ave parents?"

Ellie told him about her parents, telling him the good parts and the bad. As she talked, she grew sleepier and colder. Without thinking about it, she drew closer to him until she was lying down next to him, on the other side of Daisy and Ida. She used her arm as a pillow instead of laying her head on his shoulder, the way Daisy was, but she was close enough to be a little warmer from his body heat. Luke didn't comment on her getting closer, instead paying attention to every word she said, as if the stories about her parents were the most important thing in the whole world. Slowly, she drifted off to sleep.

"Sleep well, Ellie," Luke whispered in her ear. "I'll watch over ya."

CHAPTER 3

EVERYTHING WENT WELL ENOUGH for the next few months. The three girls managed to beg enough to have some food almost every day while Luke protected them from coppers, street gangs, and anyone else willing to do harm to three girls.

On one glorious day, Luke was approached by the rag seller. "I hurt me back and could use a hand for the day," he told Luke. "If ye work hard, and don't steal nothin', I'll give you a couple of farthings and an old blanket."

Luke readily agreed and left with the rag seller. Ellie kept watch for Ida and Daisy. She looked out for coppers, scared she would miss them. She wasn't as tall as Luke, so it was difficult for her to see over the tops of people's heads. Daisy managed to get a half penny, and a kind stranger gave Ida a half-eaten piece of fruit pie. She looked up at Ellie with a grin. "Look at this."

Ellie smiled and her stomach growled at the sight of it. She couldn't remember the last time she had a taste of something so sweet. "Don't eat it yet. Let's wait until Luke gets back." Anxiety curled in her gut. What if Luke left? What if he decided three girls were too much bother?

However, just as her thoughts started to run away from her, she felt a tap on her shoulder. She spun around in terror but relaxed as soon as she saw Luke grinning at her.

"Easy," he said, holding his hands up in surrender. Draped across one arm was a ragged, dirty blanket. It was so thin, she wondered if she could see through it. But it might as well have been the warmest, coziest quilt in the world to Ellie. Luke draped the blanket over her shoulders. "The rag seller was good on his word. One blanket and a halfpenny." He held up the dirty coin. "'Ow did you ladies make out?"

Ida displayed her half fruit pie while Daisy gave him her earnings as well. Luke smiled down at them. "We're living like dukes tonight, then," he said.

Daisy giggled, and Luke picked her up and put her on his shoulders. Ellie gently took the fruit pie from Ida and broke it into four pieces. She gave the largest piece to Ida. "For gettin' the pie in the first place," she said.

The little girl's eyes shone as she ate the sweet pie, and then the four of them went to buy some stale bread and weak tea in the market. But as they walked through the street, Ellie felt a cold wind blow through her, cutting right through the new blanket. With it came an ominous warning. Summer was ending soon. The cold weather would bring a real challenge to the four street urchins.

That night, Luke and Ellie cleared out a corner of the basement, so it was mostly clean. They piled up the rubbish around the little corner. "Smaller area makes it warmer," Luke explained to her. "Newspapers will also help. We should collect maybe a few a day—at least on the days that aren't rainin'. Wet newspapers will make us ill."

When the corner passed Luke's inspection, it was late, and Ellie's eyelids were threatening to close. She found Ida and Daisy waiting near the ladder and beckoned them over. The four of them huddled together in a pile, draping themselves in the blanket for the night. They weren't exactly warm, but at least they were dry and safe.

The cold set in as the leaves on the trees turned brown, and a winter chill filled the air. Ellie's nearly constant hunger pangs felt more intense with the cold. Not only that, but people on the streets were eager to get inside and they hurried past the beggars without sparing them a second glance. Almost no one threw them coins or food scraps anymore.

One day, Ellie was desperate. She and Luke hadn't eaten in two days. Ida and Daisy had shared a pitiful crust of bread the night before, but that was all. She felt half-crazed from the hunger running through her, and all her senses were tuned into the tantalizing aroma of meat pies coming from a market stall. Her mouth watered, and her stomach felt like a gaping hole that could never be satisfied. Luke was watching Daisy and Ida at a nearby street corner, so he wouldn't be there to help her if she got caught stealing, but she needed that meat pie.

She remembered how Luke stole bread for them all those months ago. He had been so confident about it, and no one was the wiser. There was a small crowd around the market stall and the vendor was busy serving the pies as fast as he could. Surely one couldn't hurt...

Ellie tried to walk calmly by the stall, just like Luke did. There was a lone meat pie, just far enough away from the others, where she would have a chance. She kept her eyes on the ground as she reached out and snatched the pie without looking or missing her step.

But at the last minute, the seller turned to her direction. "Hey!" he shouted, his face mottled red with rage.

Ellie took off at a run, fear coursing through her, but the man grabbed her arm with enough force to bruise her. "You little rat. I'll see you imprisoned for this."

Ellie clutched the meat pie in her free hand, as if it was a lifeline. The heat from the pie gave her enough strength to be even more daring than usual. She brought her foot up and kicked him in his most sensitive spot.

The man howled in surprise and let go of Ellie's arm. She sprinted away as fast as she could, and she didn't stop until she found Luke.

He immediately knew that something was wrong, and he reached out to grab her shoulders. "What's happened?" he asked, looking her up and down. His eyes lingered on the sight of the meat pie with blatant longing. Luke ate even less than she did, despite being bigger and taller. He had always been very thin, but these days he was looking downright skeletal.

"A-Almost got c-caught." Ellie's teeth were chattering from fear and cold. "C-Can't go into that market again."

Luke sighed and pulled her into a hug. "You need to be careful, Ellie," he said softly. "Leave the stealin' to me from now on, okay?"

She smiled, but didn't nod her head in agreement. She couldn't promise to leave the stealing to Luke, not when they didn't know what the future looked like.

Daisy and Ida came running up to them. Ida was clutching a mushroom. "This fell from a street seller's tray," she said breathlessly.

"Good job, Ida," Luke said, smiling fondly at the little girl. "Make sure you share it with Daisy. And Ellie got us a whole feast to split."

The meat pie was hardly a feast between the four of them, and it was barely lukewarm by then, but it was delicious. Ida and Daisy wolfed down their shares of the pie eagerly while Ellie took her time with her scant quarter. She savoured the taste of the meat and seasonings, with every bite feeling like a miracle. When she was finished, she licked her fingers clean, wanting as much of that good flavouring as she could get.

Luke was quiet as he ate his portion. He took barely a bite of pie for himself, and he seemed like he was almost in a trance as he ate it. "That was the best meat pie I've ever eaten," he whispered.

Ellie looked up at him and noticed his face looking a little flushed. She put her hand up against his forehead to feel it warm. Too warm. "You have a fever!"

He jerked away from her touch and gave her a smile that was more than a little forced. "The food just made my face flushed. Don't worry, Ellie, I'm as right as rain."

But he wasn't all right. Over the next few days, he got worse and worse, but he refused to take extra food. One morning, as all of them were ready to leave for a day of begging, Luke struggled to stand up and almost immediately collapsed back onto the crumpled-up blanket of the floor. Daisy cried out and tried to rush forward, but Ida held her back, even as she looked up at Ellie with wide eyes, full of fear.

The sight of Luke in this state filled Ellie with determination and fear. She couldn't let him die like her parents died. She turned to the girls. "Wait upstairs for me, but don't leave the bakery." Her tone was clipped but firm, carrying more authority than she ever used before. "Please."

The two of them scampered out of the little nook, and Ellie turned and knelt on the ground next to Luke. He looked up at her with dazed eyes. His face was flushed, but he was shivering at the same time. "Ellie–" A violent cough interrupted whatever he was going to say.

"Save your strength," she said, grabbing the blanket and tucking it over him, all the way up to his chin.

He grabbed her hand desperately. His grip felt weak, and that scared her more than she wanted to admit.

"Ellie, don't come back here," he pleaded. "Take the girls and find somewhere else to spend the night. A doorstep will keep you safe from the worst of the wind, but if you can afford it, go find a penny sit up shelter. If I get better, then I'll come find you."

A lump rose in her throat. "Don' talk like that, Luke. Ya *will* get better. I'm goin' to take care of ya."

He shook his head. "Take care of the girls. Protect them.

Don't–" He paused to cough again. Ellie couldn't help but wince at the sound. "Don't let them get ill."

"I'm not lettin' you die."

He looked at her sadly. "If it's my time, then it's my time, Ellie. Besides, the food will last longer with three instead of four."

A tear ran down her cheek. "Don't." Her voice cracked. "Yer our protector, right?"

"I can't protect ya like this."

Ellie took a deep, shuddering breath. "I'm not lettin' ya die, and that's the end of it. Get some sleep if ya can. We'll be back soon."

She climbed the ladder to find the two sisters staring at her with wide, fearful eyes. She managed a smile, but she doubted it was convincing. "It's just us three today."

"Is Luke goin' to die?" Ida asked in a small voice.

"Not if we can help it. He needs to be warm if he's goin' to get better, and he's going to need food. Everything will be fine. It must be." Her heart would probably split in two if Luke died.

Ida and Daisy gathered old newspapers which Ellie used as extra bedding for Luke. All three of them begged with renewed fervour. Daisy also rooted around in the rubbish heaps for food scraps that were fresh enough to still be edible.

Being away from Luke during the day filled Ellie with anxiety, but she had no choice. She certainly couldn't send Ida and Daisy out on their own.

That night, when they came back to the bakery, Ellie feared they would find the worst. She made Daisy and Ida stay near the ladder as she went to their corner. But Luke was still alive under the blanket and the pile of newspapers. When he heard someone approach, he sat up, brandishing his knife, his face flushed. He relaxed when he saw it was Ellie and not an attacker. "I told ya to go somewhere else," he said.

"I'm not doing that." She knelt next to him. "How are ya feeling?"

He slumped against the ground. "Tired," he mumbled, his eyes closing.

"I brought food." She carried scraps of bread and potato in her dress pocket. Now she pulled them out and tried to press one to Luke's lips, but he turned away at the last moment.

"Give it to the girls," he said. "Or eat it yourself."

"Please, Luke," she whispered. "Ya need to eat."

"Don't waste the food." He looked at her, desperation in her eyes. "You can't afford to waste food on an ill vagrant, Ellie."

"Don't say that," she said. "I need ya to live, Luke. I couldn't bear it if I lost another person to illness." She felt a tear run down her face, but she didn't care.

Luke's eyes softened, and he let her feed him the food. "I'm sorry, Ellie. I shouldn't 'ave gotten ill."

"It's 'ardly yer fault. Save yer strength so ya can get better." She fed him the rest of the food, and he didn't complain again.

Luke stayed in bed with fever and a cough for days. Ellie fed him pieces of bread and potato. The pile of newspapers helped keep Luke warm. Ellie would find more newspapers every day. She piled them on Luke and also Ida and Daisy, who were exiled to the other side of the basement at night, to keep them from getting ill.

The exhaustion weighed heavily on Ellie. Days and nights blurred together as she only focused on one goal: keeping her friends– her newfound family– alive. She barely ate or slept. When the begging didn't pay off, she would steal food from local sellers. She even got brave enough to steal ragged hats and a scarf from a rag monger.

After four long days, Luke's fever finally broke. He was still too weak to leave the cellar, but Ellie wept with relief, knowing he was getting better instead of worse.

The day after Luke's fever broke, Ellie, Ida, and Daisy were begging on the streets again. Ida came running up to Ellie with a huge grin. Her hands were clasped together in front of her. "I found this on the street," she says, parting her fingers to reveal a whole shilling. "Someone must 'ave a hole in their pocket."

Ellie could scarcely believe her eyes. A whole shilling. That would be enough for each of them to have a full meal. Having a full belly felt like a distant dream to Ellie. Not only that, but there might be enough left over to purchase a jacket for Ida. Daisy still wore Luke's jacket everywhere, but Ida would need something to keep her warm for the winter.

Ellie called Daisy over from where she was begging and Ida showed her the coin. Daisy's face lit up with excitement. "Let's get some meat pies. One for each of us!"

Ida kept the coin clutched in one hand and grabbed Ellie's other hand. Ellie grabbed Daisy's hand, and the three of them went to the meat pie cart.

They had barely gotten in line when a group of rough-looking boys ran out of nowhere. One of them knocked into Ida, and she fell to the ground.

Ellie helped her stand up. "Are you okay?"

A panicked look crossed her face. "The shilling! Where did it go?"

They searched the ground, but it was nowhere to be found. Ellie looked up just in time to see the boy who had pushed Ida to the ground, laughing with his friends and brandishing the coin. Anger rose up inside of her along with disappointment. If Luke was here, he would have gotten the coin back from that thief, if the boy had dared to take it at all. But Ellie couldn't fight an entire group of boys by herself.

Ida started to cry. "I'm so sorry. I-I didn't mean to."

Daisy patted her sister on the arm. "It's all right, Ida."

"It's not yer fault," Ellie said. "Let's just go home, yeah? Let's go see Luke." But she couldn't help but feel devastated. She was so close to having a proper meal for the first time in ages, only for it to be ripped away.

CHAPTER 4

It took the better part of a week for Luke to fully recover. By that time, winter had officially arrived in London. Blistering cold infected the basement at night, and there was little relief during the day, with powerful winds and gloomy, overcast days. Even with all four of them huddled together under newspapers and bedding, they were still shivering all through the night.

After another fruitless day of begging, Luke turned to Ellie with a grim look. "I think we need to find work and shelter, even if that's in a workhouse."

A knot twisted in her stomach, but she agreed. They had no money, and it was getting harder to steal food. That, combined with the brutal cold that suffocated the air, suggested that they wouldn't make it through winter without some help.

Instead of going back to the bakery that night, they went to a workhouse. Daisy was so exhausted from the cold and hunger that she couldn't walk. Instead, Ellie carried her while Luke carried Ida, who was just as sleepy.

Mrs. Thatcher's Workhouse wasn't far from the abandoned bakery where they lived. Ellie had walked by the building many times before, always with a feeling of trepidation. Now she was feeling that tenfold.

Luke knocked on the door and a stern-looking, middle-aged woman opened the door. She glared at all of them as if they were unwanted vermin.

"You're a sorry bunch," she said. "I'm Mrs. Thatcher, and there's no place for the little ones here. They won't be worth the food and bed space. But you two can come in if you're willing to put in a good day's work and be grateful about it."

"It has to be all of us, ma'am," Luke said. "Ellie an' I will do the work of ten kids if ya take all of us. You'll see."

She glared at him, but he met her gaze with a determined look. Finally, Mrs. Thatcher sniffed. "All right, then. You think you're worth ten kids? Prove it." She moved to the side to let them in.

The building was warm, at least warmer than outside. There was still a draft, and Ellie knew this was the type of place to carefully regulate the fires used for heat, so the air was lukewarm at best, but it was a welcome relief after being out in the frozen streets all day.

Thatcher made them wipe their feet before taking them through the workhouse. Most of the building was a huge room, full of children who were all hard at work doing laundry. They scrubbed clothing in barrels of dirty, soapy water before hanging them to dry near the fire. Others were ironing clean clothing or making repairs to torn seams and loose buttons. There were a few indifferent glances towards the newcomers, but all the children looked too tired and hungry to take any real interest in them.

"You two can sort rags," Thatcher said, pointing to Daisy and Ida. "Go on." She pointed to a large pile of rags in a cold corner of the room that was getting sorted by other children who were a bit older.

The two girls stumbled to the rag pile as fast as their weakened bodies would allow them.

The woman turned her cold gaze to the two older children. "You two will be scrubbing floors. They better be sparkling in the firelight."

"Yes, ma'am," Ellie said.

They were directed to the cleaning supplies, and they filled up buckets with cold water. Both got on their hands and knees with cleaning rags and began scrubbing the floor. They worked in silence as fast as they could, scrubbing the filth until their hands were raw and covered in soot, and their backs and legs were crying out.

They kept cleaning, well into the night, even after the other children were ushered into the mess hall for a meal of watered-down broth and a crust of bread. Ellie's stomach growled and she longed to sit on those horrible, splintering benches, crammed in with dozens of other children, just so she could drink lukewarm broth and eat a little bit of bread. At least Ida and Daisy were allowed to eat.

It was almost midnight when her body started shaking from exhaustion. As if it was moving against her will, it slowed down to a stop. Luke glanced at her without breaking pace. "If she comes back, then start scrubbing again. I'll cover for you." He started to scrub even faster, determined to do her share as well as his own.

Thatcher didn't come back to get them. They took turns scrubbing throughout the night, their arms soaked frozen from the cold water, their knees raw and aching from the kneeling, and their hands bleeding. Not only did the main room get cleaned, but so did the mess hall, the privy, and the foyer. Just before sunrise, the bell rang for the rest of the children to wake up and start their day.

Luke collapsed to the ground, his entire body shaking. His knuckles were bleeding from hours of scraping against the rough wood. His eyes fluttered shut. Ellie wasn't doing any better. Her entire body felt weak and was trembling. The hunger pangs had turned to nausea at some point in the night, and her head felt like it was spinning.

Thatcher's boots came into view as she stood over them, her arms crossed. "I should have known you two would be lazy like the others. The work of ten children indeed." She wrinkled her nose at the sight of them. "I'm not some bleeding heart, and I have no patience for two lazy teens and two young girls too weak to pull their own weight. If you can't work hard enough for room and board, then you must pay. For two pennies, you can join the others in the mess hall for breakfast, but you better not pull another stunt like this."

Ellie wanted to be angry. The floors were as clean as they could be, and the matron had to know it as well as they did. But she was too tired to be angry. She was too tired to feel anything at all.

"We don't have money, ma'am," she said, her voice little more than a whisper.

The matron didn't look surprised. Without a word, she strode into the mess hall. Shouts erupted from the room, loud enough for Luke to stir awake. He was sitting up in a daze as Mrs. Thatcher pulled Ida and Daisy out of the room by their arms. She pushed the two little girls onto the floor, next to Ellie and Luke.

"Get out!" she shouted. "All of you! There's no place for leeches like you!"

Ida and Daisy were crying as Ellie and Luke struggled to get to their feet. All of them left the workhouse with Thatcher right behind them, shouting at them the entire time. The four of them collapsed in the snow as the door slammed shut behind them.

Hot tears stung Ellie's eyes, and she tried to close them before they could fall, but she was unsuccessful. At least they managed to spend one night inside a building, even if it was the most miserable night of her life. At least Ida and Daisy managed to have one night in a bed and one meal, even if it was a paltry one.

Luke wrapped his arms around her, comforting her. "I'm sorry, Ellie," he whispered. "This was my fault. I shouldn't have fallen asleep."

"No," she said. "Ya didn't do anything wrong. She's just… a… 'orrible person!"

Luke kissed the top of her head, which gave her more comfort. "Let's go to the bakery. We can sleep the day away. It'll be warmer during the day."

They dragged themselves to their feet. Luke grabbed Ida's hand, and Ellie grabbed Daisy's as they made their way to the bakery.

But when they got there, they knew something was wrong. The door was completely off its hinges and big, muddy boot prints tracked into the old building. Alarm ran through Ellie, giving her a burst of adrenaline. She ran into the building and had to stop short when she reached the trapdoor. The ladder was in two pieces at the bottom of the hole. Rubbish, rotting animal carcasses, and debris that wasn't there before, was piled up in the basement. From the smell of it, someone had also used the basement as a privy. She didn't have to go down there to know that their precious little bedding was gone, probably stolen. There was no way this place was habitable any longer.

She collapsed on the ground, feeling despair creep into her.

Daisy grabbed her hand, looking worried. "It's okay, Ellie," she said. "We can find another place."

Luke stared down the trapdoor, looking grim. "We'll sleep in the bakery today. It's the safest place we got."

Luke and Ellie cleared a spot on the bakery floor and lay down on the dirty cobblestone, using their arms for pillows, as Ida and Daisy went out to collect newspapers to keep them warm. Luke gazed at Ellie, the exhaustion clear on his face. "I'll find a way to give ya the life ya deserve." He whispered it, as if he was saying it only to himself. "I swear it."

PART II

CHAPTER 5

Four Years Later

Spring was always Ellie's favorite time of year. The warmer weather promised more pleasant nights, and she was always grateful when winter passed and all of them were still alive.

They spent most nights huddled together in doorsteps for warmth. Sometimes they had enough money left over for Ida and Daisy to spend a night or two at a one-penny sit up shelter, but most days, the money needed to go to food and clothing.

Daisy and Ida still made money begging, but Ellie, now sixteen, didn't get a lot of attention. However, one day Luke was scavenging along the Thames and found an old street seller's tray. He found Ellie keeping watch while Daisy and Ida begged.

"Look at this," he said, brandishing the dirty tray.

She looked it over carefully. The tray was wood, and it was splintering on the sides. "It wouldn't sell for a lot," she said. "But maybe someone will give ya a farthing for it. For firewood."

He gave her a soft smile. "I was actually thinking ya could keep it."

She frowned. "Me? What for?"

"To be a street seller, of course. I can clean it up and ya can use it as if it's brand new."

She looked down. "I wouldn't know the first thing about it."

"It's easy. Buy a bunch of things in one of the big markets and sell 'em for more in one of the small local markets. Ya won't have to do mudlarkin', like me. No more running from the coppers. You'll be respectable."

Ellie couldn't imagine that, but she liked the idea. However, she shook her head. "We don't have money for that. Best to just sell it for firewood."

"I won't eat for a couple of days," Luke said. "As long as it takes." There was a determined look in his eye. "Ya deserve better than beggin' on the streets, Ellie. Maybe being a street seller will give ya the chance for something better."

Reluctantly, Ellie nodded. "All right," she said. "But if yer not eating, then I'm not eatin' neither."

He agreed to that, but he wasn't happy about it. For the next two days, Ida and Daisy were the only ones eating. It was difficult and the coins in Ellie's pocket kept taunting her into buying food, especially when her stomach growled in the middle of the night. After two days of not eating, she got up in the middle of the night and travelled to one of the bigger markets where she purchased a small supply of matches. Despite her agonizing hunger, it felt like a ray of hope.

Ellie spent twelve-hour days selling matches. Because she had to keep buying matches, she earned little more than what Daisy and Ida did while begging, but it was enough to buy food and tea.

Meanwhile, Luke would still watch out for the little girls but would also do odd jobs for some coin or food when he could and scavenge along the Thames for junk to sell. They stole food when they needed to, but luckily, they were often able to get by without resorting to thieving which eased Ellie's mind.

One March night, Ellie's feet were hurting and blistering from walking around as a street seller. Her arms and back ached, and her eyelids were heavy. The crowds of people on the street had thinned out to only a few drunks heading to their favorite tavern. She slumped against the side of a building, admitting defeat for the day.

Out of her peripheral vision, she saw movement and turned to see Luke. She smiled at the sight of him. Luke was now nineteen, and he carried their modest possessions in a ragged satchel bag. He was even taller and broader shouldered than when they had first met. Around his neck was a bright red scarf, only slightly dirty from so much time living on the street. He managed to buy it just before winter set in, and he loved it. He grinned at her with the same easy grin he always did, which made butterflies flutter in her stomach. Just a smile from him was enough to take away some of her exhaustion and pain.

Daisy and Ida were with him. Both girls were rail thin, but Ida, now ten years old, was starting to grow tall. It wouldn't be long before she would need a new dress. At least Daisy could wear Ida's old clothes.

"Guess what?" Daisy said, grinning up at Ellie. "I petted a dog."

"You did?" She smiled.

"It was a little fluffy dog, and it wagged its tail really fast. I wanted to give it a piece of bread, but Ida said no."

Daisy pouted, but Ellie was relieved. They barely had enough to keep the worst of the hunger pangs away. The last thing they could do was give precious food to stray animals.

"I earned a few pennies today," Luke said. "I managed to get some work at the docks for the day. We have enough for food or for Ida and Daisy to go to the penny sit-up."

Ida pouted. "I don't want to go to the sit up. They just make you sit on 'orrible benches all night and they don't let ya sleep."

"A night inside a warm building is better than outside," Ellie reminded her. The penny sit-up shelters weren't that warm, but they were warm enough where Ida and Daisy didn't have to worry about freezing to death in the middle of the night in winter.

"The nights are gettin' warmer," Luke said. "I'm bettin' we don't need a penny sit-up tonight. Let's get some food and some tea before the market closes."

Ida and Daisy cheered and ran ahead. Luke and Ellie hung back a little ways but kept them in their sights. He took the seller's tray from her, studying the matches left. "Slow day?"

She nodded. "I can only spare a halfpenny today, if I want to buy more matches." She could feel the coins jingling in her dress pocket, tempting her to spend it all on food and hot tea, or even shoes and stockings for the girls. But she needed to hold herself back if she wanted to buy some more matches to sell.

"Use that halfpenny to buy yourself something," Luke said. "You could get a day-old muffin with it, or maybe even a slice of plum pudding."

She smiled at the thought but shook her head. "You were lucky at the docks today. Tomorrow, maybe not." She would rather save what she could so Daisy and Ida could each have at least something to eat every day. She hoped, one day, she and Luke would be able to make enough for the four of them to have a place together in the slums, a place they would actually call home. She dreamed of cooking hot meals for them over her own cooker and mending their clothes near the fire. Maybe Daisy and Ida could even take time to learn their letters and arithmetic so they could get decent jobs. It was merely a fantasy, but some days, when her feet were hurting, and her hands were numb with cold, it was the only thing that kept her going.

"You never get anything for yourself," Luke said. "Even on good days."

"Not all days are good," she said. "I'd rather keep us alive."

He looked sad, but he knew she was right. He sighed and took off his scarf and wrapped it around her neck. She looked up at him, surprised. "What's this for?"

"Because I want to," he said. "You're cold, I know ya are. And I wannna take care of ya."

A lump rose in her throat at the small gesture of kindness. "I don't know what I would do without ya," she whispered.

He smiled, his eyes soft with affection and something else, something Ellie couldn't identify. "You'll never have to know. I ain't goin' anywhere. I promise." He looked down and took a step away from her. A slight blush dusted across his cheeks, making his smile look downright bashful. "An' one of these days, I'll marry ya."

Ellie laughed, but part of her longed to be married to Luke, one of the kindest men she had ever known.

They reached the market, where each of them was able to buy a cup of tea and split a loaf of bread. The tea was so weak, it barely had any flavour, but Ellie didn't care. The days might be getting warmer, but the winter always left a chill deep inside her. Warm tea helped chase it out a little.

When they finished the tea and bread, they left the market. Now that Ellie was slightly warmer and the worst of her hunger pangs had subsided, she felt peaceful, even happy. And the weather would only be getting warmer, which meant good days to come.

The four of them walked to a church which had a large enough doorstep for all of them to take shelter in, and huddle together. They all sat down, with Luke keeping Ellie's seller's tray and matches safely stowed away in the satchel. He pulled out an old rag that served as a blanket for Daisy and Ida. They pulled the filthy blanket around themselves and huddled up against Luke for as much warmth as they could muster. Luke looked at Ellie and held out his arm, inviting her to come closer.

She felt her cheeks grow warm as she leaned against his shoulder. He wrapped his arm around her, enveloping her in heat. They'd slept nights like this hundreds of times before, but with every passing night, she loved it more and more. She loved just being close to Luke, even if it was only to share warmth. She closed her eyes and let herself drift off to sleep.

She woke up the next morning by strong hands roughly pulling her up. She heard Daisy and Ida both scream and looked to see them being held by a man each. Terror gripped her, and she tried to struggle against her own captor, who laughed. His breath smelled like rotting tobacco, and she wanted to gag.

"Ain't you a pretty thing," he breathed in her ear. "Scrawny and filthy, but I know plenty of men who wouldn't give a damn."

"Let them go," said Luke. He was looking at the men, anger and fear in his eyes.

The man holding Ida froze and stared at him. "I know you," he said. "Luke, right? I thought you were bloody dead, man."

Luke's lip curled. "Jack." He took his knife out of his pocket, ready to fight. "You don't want to do this."

The man holding Daisy laughed. "What are ya gonna do against the three of us? We're holding your girls."

"I won't let ya take 'em," he said. "Ya might get the better of me in the end, but I reckon I can get an eye or two– maybe even stab one of ya in the gut so ya can bleed out in the street. Is that worth the risk for three starving girls?"

Ellie felt dread rise inside of her. Unfortunately, she knew it *was* worth the risk. She didn't know exactly what they would do to her, but she knew there was money in kidnapping girls no one would miss. She didn't know where they went, but she knew it was a fate worse than death.

Daisy cried out as the man gripped her arm harder. Luke flinched at the sound. "Take me instead," he blurted out. "Ya can sell me at the docks."

All the air left Ellie at once. *No.*

"To 'ell with this mess," Ellie's captor said. "We can take all of 'em."

Jack's expression was speculative as he looked at Luke. Ellie remembered Luke mentioning he used to spend time with a group of boys until they started kidnapping people on the street. Jack must have been one of those boys. Luke must have made quite an impression if Jack remembered him all these years later.

"No," Jack said finally. "Luke was always a fighter an' he could give us a good lickin' if he wanted. We can get a good price for 'im at the docks, without gettin' bruised."

"Let 'em go, and I'll put the knife down," Luke said.

Ellie felt tears well up in her eyes. *No, Luke! Please, ya can't do this. We need ya. I need ya.*

"No funny business," Ellie's captor said. "Or I'll come back for this one and enjoy 'er personally." His grip on her arm tightened, and she flinched.

The rage was evident on Luke's face, but he nodded.

"Luke," Ellie whimpered. "Don't do this. Please."

He looked at her, a thousand emotions playing out over his face, including longing, hurt, and grief. "I'll find ya, Ellie," he said. "I promise."

Jack agreed to let Ida and Daisy run away, but Ellie was forced to watch Luke put the knife on the ground and put his hands up in the air. Only then did the man holding her arm loosen his grip. She stumbled away from him and turned around, prepared to fight.

"Get out of here, Ellie!" Luke's voice was sharp. "Look after the girls."

Reluctantly, she backed away, down the street. Silently, she pleaded for Luke to fight, to escape, but he didn't even try. He let the men grab him and pull him down the street.

Ellie found Ida and Daisy around the corner. When they saw her face, they knew Luke was gone, and they dissolved into tears. Ellie hugged them close to her, wishing more than anything that she could break down and cry too, but she couldn't. She needed to remain strong and take care of them, even though it felt like her heart was torn into a million pieces.

There was nothing they could do for Luke. Ellie and the girls went to the docks and asked anyone who might listen to them for information. No one would talk to them for a while, and others didn't have any information. Eventually, one of the sailors could give them information.

"I remember seeing a boy fittin' that description," he said. "And I know Jack and his lot. They come down here too much."

"Do you know where they took Luke?" Ellie asked. "I need to find him."

"I'm sorry, miss," the man said, his eyes soft with sympathy. "But if I'm right– and I think I am– then Jack sold yer friend to Captain Rowe, captain of the *Northern Spirit*. He's a nasty fellow, that Rowe. Not willin' to pay his crew one penny."

Ellie's heart leaped to her throat. "Where are they?" She didn't know how she would help Luke escape Captain Rowe, but she would find a way.

"They already left port, miss," the sailor said. "I'm sorry, I am. But this sort of thing happens all the time down here. It's a nasty business, it is. Ya might as well give up. Ya ain't gonna find yer friend."

His words made her feel like she was punched in the gut. Luke was gone, and there was nothing she could do to make him come back. She fell to her knees, not even noticing Ida and Daisy kneeling next to her.

It was too easy to remember his smiling face from the day before. "I ain't goin' anywhere. I promise. An' one of these days, I'll marry ya." Her heart felt like it was ripped into two pieces.

She didn't know how long she sat on the docks, lost in her grief, but when she finally looked around at her surroundings again, the sailor was gone, and Ida and Daisy were looking at her with frightened faces.

"There's still some daylight," she forced herself to say. "Maybe we can earn some coin. You two with beggin' and me with..." She realized Luke still had the satchel on him when he was taken– the satchel with her matches and seller's tray. Fear gripped her, and she had to take deep breaths to calm herself down. *Ya gotta calm down, Ellie. Ya gotta stay strong for the girls.* The voice in her head sounded a lot like Luke's.

For the rest of the day, Daisy and Ida begged for coin and food while Ellie kept an eye out for coppers. They kept begging until well past sunset but only received a couple of farthings for their efforts. They gave the coins to Ellie, who put them in her pocket, with the meagre amount of money she was going to use to buy more matches to sell. She ended up buying a piece of bread for Ida and Daisy to share, but nothing for herself. For the first time in a long time, she wasn't hungry. The grief inside of her was too strong.

That night, they found an abandoned factory. The inside was empty, except for rubbish, but the outside was in good repair.

The three of them huddled inside together. Ellie missed Luke's warmth and comforting presence. She missed the feeling she got from his arms wrapping around her.

Ida sniffled, even though she tried to muffle the sound, and Ellie put her hand on the little girl's head.

"It's all right," she said quietly. "Ya can cry if ya want."

As Ida sobbed, Daisy looked up at Ellie with a fearful expression. "He'll come back, won't he? Those ships always come back, don't they?"

Ellie managed a trembling smile, even though everything felt horrible. "He told me he would come back. He promised. Luke keeps his promises."

Daisy nodded. "When he comes back, I'm going to give him the biggest hug. Then I'll buy him a fruit pie."

Ellie hugged the girls tightly in her arms all night, as if she was scared to let them go.

CHAPTER 6

Months went by. Spring turned to summer, and summer began to lose its warmth as autumn came around the corner. Ida and Daisy spent their time begging or scavenging on the Thames while Ellie went back to selling matches, this time without a tray. They all made a meagre living, but they managed to make do.

But as the nights grew colder, their paltry, threadbare clothing and newspapers weren't enough to keep them warm, even in the abandoned factory, which at least sheltered them from the worst of the wind. One day, as they woke up with the sunrise, Daisy sneezed.

"Are you getting ill?" Ellie asked, feeling her forehead. Daisy was a little warm, but she wasn't quite feverish yet.

Ida looked at her sister, worry clear in her eyes. "It's okay if ya are. Ellie will nurse you back to health, just like she did with Luke. Don't ya be worrying."

Ellie smiled and nodded as pain lanced through her heart, whenever she thought about Luke. Whenever she could, she would go to the docks to see if there was any word about Captain Rowe. But she never heard anything about him or Luke.

"We'll get you some hot tea today. That will fix ya right up. Ida, can ya go scavenging alone today?"

Ida nodded. "Of course. I'm old enough."

Ellie smiled. "Good. I'll keep Daisy with me today then. It won't do to have her crawling through filth if she's ill. Bad enough she has to be out in the cold."

Ida went to scavenge along the Thames while Ellie walked along the streets of London, clutching Daisy's hand while trying to sell matches to anyone who looked her way. There were a few takers, but not a lot. At the end of the day, she counted her money, which was only a few pennies. It looked like she would skip supper tonight. It was more important Daisy had food and hot tea.

Daisy had been uncharacteristically quiet all day, and now, as they stood still at the edge of a market, the little girl sat on the ground and leaned against Ellie's leg.

Ida ran up to them, looking at her sister with concern. "Ya all right, Daisy?"

The little girl coughed, which made anxiety curl inside Ellie's chest. She was definitely getting ill. "Did ya get any money, Ida?" She tried to keep the alarm out of her voice.

Ida gave her a dirty halfpenny. "This is all they'd give me. Only found a few bits of iron."

Ellie nodded. "Button up Daisy's jacket, will ya?"

Ida quickly went to button it up. It was the same jacket that Luke gave Daisy all those years ago. Daisy had grown up a little since then, but the jacket was still quite big on her. Ellie hoped it would be enough to keep her warm and comfortable.

Ellie bought hot tea for Ida and Daisy and had just enough left over for a stale loaf of bread. She took none for herself and gave Daisy the largest portion. Ida didn't protest.

They went back to the factory for the night, where Ellie piled a lot of newspapers on Daisy, hoping to keep her warm throughout the night. Food and warmth were how she nursed Luke back to health all those years ago. Maybe they would protect Daisy today.

But when they woke up the next morning, Daisy was worse. Her face was flushed with a horrible fever, and her eyes were dazed as she looked around. Ida knelt next to her sister and grabbed her hand.

"Daisy?" she said. "Can ya get up, Daisy? We can get ya some food. A fruit pie! I won't take any, honest. Ya can have it all." Her voice cracked at the sound of it.

Daisy looked in her sister's direction, but her eyes didn't quite focus. "Ida," she said softly. "Going to pet the doggies today."

"Yes, that's right," Ida said. "We'll pet all the stray dogs. I'll even let ya feed them a bit of bread. But ya need to get better. Please, Daisy." A tear fell down her cheek, and she looked up at Ellie. "She'll be all right, won't she? She just needs some sleep and some food."

A lump formed in Ellie's throat as she looked at Daisy. She couldn't form the words to reassure Ida because she wasn't sure herself. And she hated herself for that failure. She couldn't even comfort the girls. Luke told her to take care of them, and she couldn't even do that. She wanted to sit down and cry, but she couldn't. She had to do something to help. Anything.

"I'm going to get medicine," she said. "Stay here, Ida. Don't leave her side and keep her warm."

She left the abandoned factory, trying to forget how much Daisy looked like her mother had during her last days. How her mother, face flushed with fever, talked deliriously about different things. She muttered on and on about how sweet Ellie looked as a baby and how she would knit Ellie a hat for winter. And now Daisy was talking about petting dogs. Her stomach twisted.

She couldn't let Daisy die, not like this.

She stopped and hid in a corner to count out how much money she had. It was a meagre amount, but maybe it would be enough for medicine. She ran to the nearest apothecary and went inside. A stern looking man was behind the counter. He glowered at her.

"I have nothing for you, vagrant," he said.

"Please, I can pay," she said. "My sister is very ill. She has a bad fever, and I scared she won't live long. Do ya have something for a fever?"

He sighed. "Of course, I have something for a fever." He pulled out a glass vial of liquid. "This will ease the fever and keep her comfortable, but it's not cheap."

"How much can I get for this?" She dumped all of her coins on the counter.

He looked at the dirty coins in disgust. "This is nothing."

"Please, it's all I have. I'll take what I can, even just a drop. Or-or I can pay ya back. All of the money I make will go to ya."

He glared at her. "As if I believe ya. You're all just a bunch of lyin' thieves." He put the medicine away. "This would be wasted on your sister anyway. She needs to be clean, warm, and comfortable, and I doubt you're capable of providing that. It's a mercy to everyone if she dies, including herself. Who wants to be a street urchin?"

Tears sprang to Ellie's eyes. "Daisy is the sweetest girl in the world, and she deserves to live, you 'orrid man! Now please tell me how much do I need for the medicine?"

"Two shillings. But I doubt a wretch like you could even get one before it's too late."

The tears start to fall down Ellie's face because she knew it was true. She's never held more than one shilling at once. "Is there anything I can do, sir? There must be somethin'. I'll do anythin'. I know how to clean real good. Or I can run errands for ya. Please."

A flicker of something that resembled sympathy entered his face for a moment before he turned away, his expression cold again. "Keep her as warm and clean as ya can. Nature will take its course, and it might be merciful."

Ellie nodded and left, feeling absolute despair. She gathered as many newspapers from the streets as she could. Less than a day old, the newspapers were as clean as she could manage. She went back to the factory to see Ida crying as she held Daisy's hand. She looked up at Ellie, hope entering her face for a moment, before she saw Ellie's grim expression. Then grief took over.

"We need to keep her clean and warm," Ellie said, setting down the newspapers. "Help me spread these out on the ground. And we don't need to be cryin' now. There's a lot of hope yet. We're gonna take good care of 'er."

Ellie felt horrible lying to Ida as she tried to keep Ida from despair. Truth was, Ellie felt that same despair, but it wasn't going to do Daisy any good.

They spread the newspapers out on the dirty ground and moved Daisy onto the makeshift bed. Daisy barely reacted as they set her down. Ellie gave Ida the money. "Get some food for 'er," she said. "Whatever this money can buy." She wouldn't have any money left to replenish her paltry stock of matches, but it didn't matter. What was the point of selling matches if she couldn't even keep her family alive?

"Come on, Daisy," she said after Ida left, her voice breaking. "You need to stay alive. Luke will be back soon, and ya need to give him the biggest hug, right? Ya said ya would give him the biggest hug."

"Luke," Daisy whispered, her eyes fluttering shut. "Nice."

"That's right, honey. He is nice. He gave ya this jacket, remember?" Carefully, Ellie unbuttoned the jacket and pulled it off her. Daisy shivered from the cold air touching her skin and Ellie felt a pang of guilt. "Just for a moment, Daisy, I promise."

As gently as she could, Ellie took off Daisy's dress, which was dirty from the mud and grime of living on the street. Ellie used Luke's scarf to wipe the worst of the filth off Daisy's hands, arms, and legs. Ellie would sell her soul for a bowl of warm water, so she could truly keep Daisy clean.

When Daisy was as clean as she was going to get, Ellie covered her with Luke's jacket and more newspapers. She put her hand on Daisy's forehead, and the hot skin almost burned her. Daisy sighed and leaned into her touch.

"Cold," she said, a small smile in her voice.

By this time, Ida was back with a meat pie. Ellie's stomach growled fiercely from the scent of it, and she knew Ida would be in a similar state, but this pie was all for Daisy, and they both knew it. She moved out of the way.

"Daisy, Ida's got something for you. A special treat."

Ida knelt next to her sister and held up the meat pie so Daisy could smell it. Daisy shook her head. "Not hungry."

"Please, honey, you need to eat," Ellie said. "Just a little bit. You need to grow up big and strong, right? We want you all better by the time Luke gets back home to us."

They managed to coax Daisy to take a small bite, and then another before she refused to take any more. She curled up on her side, her eyes closed, as she drifted off into sleep. Ellie and Ida stayed by her side while she slept. After a few hours, she woke up and ate some more of the pie, but she ended up vomiting it onto one of the newspapers. Ellie quickly cleaned it up and somehow managed to do it without crying.

"Sorry," Daisy whispered weakly. "Made a mess."

"It's all right, honey," Ellie whispered. "Make as much of a mess as you want. Just get better."

Daisy looked up at her with her flushed face. Her expression twisted as she coughed before she looked at Ellie, then Ida. "Love you," she whispered, before falling back to sleep.

Ida held her sister, openly sobbing. "I love you, Daisy. Please, please, wake up. I need ya, please. Ya can't leave us."

Ellie shut her eyes, but the tears came anyway. She covered her face in her hands and sobbed silently.

She must have dozed without realizing it, because she woke up with a start to Ida screaming.

"Daisy!" Ida shouted, shaking her sister's form. "Wake up, Daisy! Please! Don't leave us! Wake up!"

Ellie stared in horror at Daisy's limp form. Her mouth was open, in almost an awestruck expression, but her eyes were glazed over, staring at nothing. Ellie's throat nearly closed. Daisy would never look at either of them again, she would never pet another dog, and she would never be able to hug Luke again. She was gone.

Ellie had failed. They'd lost Daisy.

Ellie and Ida hugged Daisy's body close as the two girls cried openly.

CHAPTER 7

DAISY WAS BURIED in a pauper's grave. The sweet little girl, who was always quick with a smile, deserved so much more than that, but there was nothing they could do about it. Ida had spent all of their money on a meat pie for Daisy, and they had nothing else.

Both were devastated beyond words. They didn't go back to the factory– they couldn't bear it when that was the place Daisy had died. Instead, they spent the nights huddled together in different doorsteps. Neither of them got a lot of sleep. Instead, they spent their nights crying, missing Daisy and Luke. Their days were spent in a fog of grief and exhaustion. Without Daisy there, everything felt a million times harder for Ellie. Just getting up with the sunrise and begging was almost impossible. If she didn't have to take care of Ida, she probably wouldn't have bothered at all, and instead let nature take its course with her the way it had for Daisy.

Ida didn't speak, and she only moved when Ellie told her to. She ate food scraps, but only enough to keep herself alive. Ellie couldn't even tempt her with promises of fresh fruit and hot tea.

A week after Daisy was buried, Ellie woke up with the sunrise. Ida was sitting up shivering, staring off into the distance. Her thin face was looking even more gaunt and the dark circles under her eyes were even more pronounced. She wore Daisy's jacket now. It should have been burned with the rest of Daisy's clothing, because of the fever, but neither Ida nor Ellie had the heart to give it up.

Ellie's heart twisted at the sight of her friend– her sister in everything except blood. Even though grief and pain pulled at her, she knew she had to summon whatever remaining shreds of strength she had to keep them both alive.

"I'm going to find a job," she told Ida. "A proper one this time."

She was seventeen now, and she was as determined to be as hard a worker as anyone else. Winter was coming soon, and she needed to make sure they survived. Surely God would have mercy on her after all she'd suffered. Surely, he would lead her to something—something more than this aching emptiness and hopeless despair.

Ida only nodded, not really hearing the words. She'd heard them before and all to no avail. Ellie bit the inside of her lip. Not this time. This time she wouldn't stop until she found something.

Ida hugged her knees to her chest and closed her eyes as she leaned against the doorway of an old, abandoned building. Ellie knew she wouldn't move from her spot unless a copper told her to leave.

Ellie stood up and walked through the street. She knocked on shop doors and factory doors, asking if they had any work for her. Most turned her away with an insult or two. Some of them threatened to call the police on her if she kept causing problems. The harsh words didn't deter her. She didn't have the capacity to feel much worse than she already did. In truth, she was numb.

Without feeling much hope, she knocked on the door of a dress shop. A surly looking woman answered and looked Elic up and down. "What do you want?"

"A job, ma'am," she said.

The woman grunted. "You? You're a dirty ragamuffin. Do you know what kind of shop this is? Can you sew? Can you use a machine?"

Ellie swallowed hard. She did her best to look intelligent. "No, ma'am, but I'm a fast learner, and I'll work hard. Real hard. No one works harder."

The woman stared at her for a long time before looking inside the shop. She sighed. "I could use the extra help. Two of my girls got themselves pregnant last month."

She backed away from the door. "All right, you can come in, and I'll teach you how to use the machine. I ain't payin' you today, but if you can work as quick as the others by the end of the day, then tomorrow you can begin work for two shillings a week."

There was a greedy gleam in her eye, and Ellie had a hunch that two shillings a week was far less than what the other workers got paid, but she wasn't in a position to quibble. Besides, two shillings would have meant the difference between life and death to Daisy.

Ellie nodded. "Thank ya, ma'am."

Her new employer, Mrs. Long, was tough but fair. She took her time teaching Ellie how to properly operate and care for the sewing machine in a room with twenty other girls, all busy with their work. Ellie felt lost and bewildered though she did her best to hide it. And steadily, she caught on. She knew it might work out when she glimpsed a knowing look in Mrs. Long's eyes.

By the end of the day, Ellie was able to sew pieces of a blouse or a dress as quickly as any of them.

Mrs. Long cast a gratified eye over the small pile of finished clothing on Ellie's table. "It's adequate, child. I want you back here tomorrow morning at six o'clock sharp. Work begins at six and ends at eight o'clock at night. You have fifteen minutes at noon for lunch. You'll work every day except Sundays, and if you miss a day, then do not bother coming back, understand?"

"Yes, ma'am," Ellie said meekly.

"Off you go, then."

Ellie left the factory, exhausted but feeling strangely all right. The hard work had distracted her from her grief, and although she wasn't content, not by a long shot, the pain inside of her was muted.

She went to the nearest market, where some sellers were closing for the night. She watched as a baker dumped two old bread loaves into a rubbish bin before going back into his bakery. She went to the bin and immediately fished them out. They were a little dirty, slightly burnt, and incredibly stale, but it was food which she and Ida desperately needed. She tossed the dirty and burnt bits back into the bins before going to the doorstep where Ida waited for her. She handed one of the loaves to her.

"I got a job at a factory," she told Ida. "I'm going to be gone a long time, but we'll have money for food, maybe even for shelter some nights."

Ida nodded, but didn't react any further. She held the bread limply in her hand.

"Come on, Ida," Ellie whispered. "I can't lose you, too."

The eleven-year-old girl looked at Ellie with eyes red from crying. "I miss her."

Her voice was hoarse and scratchy, barely above a whisper. The sound of it made Ellie want to cry.

"I know you do," she said. "I miss her too. I miss her dearly. But she wouldn't want us to be miserable, not Daisy. She always did everything she could to cheer us up. Let's think of the better days. Let's think of her laughing and teasing. Let's think of how much she liked pettin' them dogs."

Tears continued to fall down Ida's cheeks. "It's my fault," she said, sobbing. "I complained so much about the penny sit ups. Maybe if she had more warm nights, she wouldn't have gotten ill."

"No, none of that." Ellie pulled the girl in her arms. "It's no one's fault, do you hear me? It's just a 'orrible, 'orrible thing. That's all." She closed her eyes as she held Ida tightly in her arms. They cried together until Ellie insisted they stop and eat their bread.

Because they'd already spent more than one night in that doorstep, they wandered until they found another. This one was a bit more hidden, and Ellie felt safer there. Both were exhausted and fell asleep almost immediately.

Ellie arrived at the clothing shop a few minutes before six, still feeling exhausted and thinking about the small piece of bread in her dress pocket, which would be her lunch. She already couldn't wait until the end of the week, when she would receive two shillings. It would be enough to give her and Ida a bit of food every day for the next week, if she was careful.

Mrs. Long didn't greet her as she entered, except to say, "Wash your hands, child. I won't have you getting the clothing dirty."

Ellie did as she was told and got to work. None of the other girls talked to her or even to each other. Instead, they all concentrated and worked in silence to make sure they met their quotas so they could work another day.

At noon, Ellie stood up and stretched a little before eating her bread. She wasn't used to sitting for so long at a time, especially indoors and with clean hands. Despite her entire body aching from the work, and her fingers freezing, this place felt like a luxury compared to walking the streets of London outside, selling matches. She couldn't help but worry about Ida. What was the girl doing all day? She likely did some begging, but Ellie fretted that she was mostly crying, missing her sister.

When the day was finally over, she left the factory. Her entire body felt stiff, and her hands ached, but she still felt reluctant to leave the shop and go back outside. However, she needed to find Ida. With some luck, she would be able to scavenge or steal some food for the two of them.

When she went to the doorstep of the abandoned building they'd slept at the night before, Ida wasn't there. Panic hit her fast, and Ellie turned around, hoping she could find the girl quickly.

"Ida!" she called into the crowded London street. "Ida!"

How could she find her? What if she had been kidnapped or arrested or worse?

"Ellie?"

She turned around to see Ida standing on the street, clutching some bread. Sheer relief knocked air back into Ellie's lungs. She ran up to Ida and pulled her into a hug. "I was so worried," she said. "Where did you go?"

"I went to get food," Ida said, holding up the loaf of bread. "If you're workin', then I should work too. I did some begging. Daisy wouldn't want me to starve."

"No," Ellie said, kissing Ida on the top of her head, just like her mother used to do for her. "Definitely not."

They huddled together on the doorstep and shared food. Ellie was so tired, she fell asleep only a few seconds after finishing the last crumb of bread.

Morning came too soon for her. She woke up shivering, feeling as if she hadn't slept at all. Half-heartedly, she parted from Ida's sleeping form, feeling more than a little anxiety from having to leave her again for the day. She would have to get used to leaving Ida by herself if she was going to keep this job.

She went to the clothing shop, her stomach hurting from hunger. She didn't even have any lunch this time to look forward to. Mrs. Long only talked to her to correct a mistake in a blouse she was sewing together.

"Honestly, if you keep making careless mistakes like that, then I'm just going to have to dock your pay."

"I'm sorry, ma'am, I'll do better." Ellie was careful not to make any more mistakes for the rest of the day.

At the end of her shift, she walked out and was immediately assaulted by a brutal, winter wind. She shivered and pulled her scarf up to cover her face. Luke's scarf.

She wondered where he was now. Was he even still alive? She hadn't visited the docks once since Daisy had died. With a pang of sadness, she realized she wouldn't be able to go there again. There simply wouldn't be enough time with such long hours while working. Perhaps she could go on her one day off.

What does it matter? Captain Rowe's ship has never come back to port. For all you know, the ship was crashed at sea.

She put those thoughts away. She couldn't keep thinking about Luke. It just made her heart ache too much. She had to stay strong for Ida.

Ida didn't have any luck begging or scavenging for food that day, so they went to bed hungry. Ellie couldn't sleep because of the aches in her stomach, but she managed to drag herself away to go to work the next morning.

The rest of the week passed by in a blur, with Ellie thinking about very little except the two shillings at the end of the week. Sometimes Ida managed to find a scrap or two of food for them, but the food did little to ease Ellie's stomach. Somehow, she barely managed to keep from getting reprimanded by Mrs. Long, and at the end of the week, the woman gave her two shilling coins at the end of her shift.

"Off you go," she said. "Remember, tomorrow's Sunday. Don't show up here."

Ellie stared down at the coins, feeling numb. This was the money she had worked so hard for, but she couldn't even muster up a scrap of joy at the sight of it.

The woman looked at her with more than a little impatience. "Off you go," she said again, clearly dismissing Ellie.

Ellie left the shop in a daze, clutching the two shillings to herself as she went to the doorstep she and Ida were calling home these days. The other girl was nowhere to be found, so Ellie decided to go to the nearest market before it shut down for the night. Normally, she would wait for Ida, but she was too hungry. All she had eaten for the past two days were scraps of potato Ida pulled out of a rubbish heap.

On her way to the market, she heard a scream coming from a nearby alley. Her heart leaped to her throat as she realized it sounded like Ida. Turning around in a panic, she raced to the alley just in time for Ida to come running out of it, being chased by three older boys. Ellie ran after her, hurrying to stuff her two shillings into her pocket on the way.

Terror at seeing Ida about to be attacked gave her a burst of adrenaline she didn't know she was capable of. She ran forward and put herself between Ida and the boys. "Go!" she screamed at them.

The gang of boys were probably fifteen or sixteen. Older than Ida, but younger than she was. However, they were a rough-looking group with scars and sneers on their faces.

"That witch was in our territory," one of the boys said. "We don't take kindly to trespassers."

"Well, she won't be back," Ellie cried. "Now leave before I call the coppers on ya!"

It was an empty threat. She had gone this long without talking to the policemen, and she certainly wasn't going to start now. But the boys' faces paled, and they ran off.

Ellie turned to Ida, whose face was tearstained.

"I didn't know," she said, her voice trembling. "No one bothered me yesterday when I went through the rubbish."

"It's all right," Ellie said. "It just means it's time to find some new rubbish bins to look through. But not tonight. Tonight, we can go to the market!"

She reached into her pocket, and her heart stopped when she felt only a single coin in there. She must have dropped one of the coins when she hastily put them in her pocket. Tears sprang to her eyes as she thought about how hard she worked only for a moment of distracted carelessness to take it all away. Even though she had felt very little happiness at receiving the coins, she certainly felt the full devastation of losing one of them.

"Ellie?" Ida's voice was cautious and a little worried.

She managed a shaky smile. "I seem to have lost one of the coins," she said. "No matter. A shilling will be enough for us to get through the week. Let's go before the market closes."

They shared a cup of weak tea and a small piece of bread for dinner before drifting off to sleep on their doorstep.

WEEKS WENT on in a blur of stress-infused monotony. Ellie worked long hours for her meagre pay while Ida scavenged in rubbish piles, careful to stay away from those horrible boys. On Sundays, Ellie rested so she could save her strength for the long days ahead. Two shillings a week was enough to make sure they could eat at least something every day, and Ellie was able to buy better shoes for Ida and a coat for herself from the rag seller. Both the shoes and coat were tattered, but they were necessary to help them survive the winter.

Late night on Saturday, Ellie received her pay from Mrs. Long. One of the other girls, Amelia, smiled as she received her own pay (a few shillings more than Ellie). She turned to Ellie.

"Aren't you excited for tomorrow? Do you have any plans? I'm goin' to church, and then to the market."

Ellie smiled at the young woman. Even though she wasn't close to any of the girls at the shop, she occasionally exchanged pleasantries with them during the lunch break or after work. Amelia was usually in good spirits, despite the gruelling work, so Ellie liked talking to her. "

No plans," she said. She didn't want to reveal too much to Amelia, in case the other woman discovered that Ellie didn't go home to a flat in the slums like most of the other women. She was actually thinking about treating both her and Ida to a night at the two-penny hangover. For two pennies, they could spend the night sitting in benches in a warm room and leaning over a rope while they slept. It was slightly more comfortable than the penny sit-up, and a night out of the brutal winter elements would do them some good.

"You know, I know next to nothing about you, Ellie. Do you have a family? A fellow, perhaps?"

She thought about Luke for a moment and felt a pang of sadness. "Not anymore."

Sympathy touched Amelia's eyes. "Oh, you poor thing. Forgive me, I didn't realize you were a widow."

Ellie was startled, but she shook her head. She supposed it was an easy assumption to make now. Years of living on the street gave her an aura and face older than seventeen. Perhaps she should be surprised that more people didn't take her for someone in her early twenties.

"Oh no, I'm not a widow. There was just this boy a long time ago." How long had it been since she lost Luke? A few months? A year? It felt like a lifetime ago. "He was taken from me."

"That's so awful. But maybe you'll find another, yeah? Of course, good men are hard to find."

"Luke was a good man," she said. "The best, actually." A hard lump rose in her throat. "I should go. Enjoy yer day off, Amelia."

She hurried from the shop, trying to stop the pain and sadness welling up inside of her. She cursed herself as she walked swiftly down the street. She had no business indulging these thoughts. Luke was gone. Daisy was gone. All her dreams for the future– of having a home where she could cook meals and tend to the fire– were gone. All that mattered was keeping herself and Ida alive, one day at a time.

CHAPTER 8

Both Ida and Ellie survived the winter. As the weather warmed without either of them falling ill, some of Ellie's anxiety eased. She would gladly take working in the stuffy shop, where she would spend hours sweating and sewing, if it meant there was no risk for either of them freezing to death during the night.

One Sunday, Ellie was busy counting her coins and trying to plan what food to buy. It was warm enough where they didn't have to spend money on the two penny hangovers, which meant more food per day. Maybe she would even be able to take a bit of lunch to work. Not a lot, because she didn't want to eat more food than Ida, but a small bite of bread and even a little cheese would be welcome after so much work.

Ida came running up to her, grinning, and holding something in her hands. "Look what I have," she said. Carefully, she opened her hand to show a metal brooch, embedded with jewels.

Ellie's eyes widened as she took it. "Where did you get this?"

The pin attached to the brooch was damaged and the metal was a little rusty, but she was sure this was the most valuable item she had ever seen, much less held in her hands.

"I found it in the rubbish. Don't know how it got there. Who would throw out a pretty little thing like this?"

"Does not matter. What matters now is we have it." Ellie picked herself up, stretching. Her body felt stiff from sitting for so long and sore from all the work the day before. "Let's hurry to the pawn shop before it closes."

The nearest pawn shop was run by a man known for being a sly businessman who would haggle his own mother out of her fine silver. But he also did not care much where his merchandise came from.

Ellie walked in, holding up the brooch before the store owner told her to leave. "Good afternoon, sir. I would like to sell this."

He looked at her suspiciously. "How did the likes of you get a piece like that?"

"A rubbish pile, sir," Ida said from behind Ellie, beaming.

The man raised an eyebrow and grunted. "If it was in the rubbish, then it was probably not worth anything." But he held out his hand for the brooch and examined it carefully.

"The metal is all rusted," he said. "And it's damaged. But I suppose the jewels could be salvaged. They're not the most precious, mind you. No fine ladies would be caught dead wearing these jewels, and the design is horribly out of fashion." He sighed and put the brooch on the counter. "I suppose I can give ya a shilling for it."

Adrenaline and happiness surged through Ellie at the thought of a whole extra shilling. They would be able to get more food. Maybe even some meat and cheese. Her stomach growled at the thought, and she knew Ida's jaw had dropped at the amount of money, and the possibility.

But something inside Ellie held back. She knew this pawnbroker was sly, so if he was offering a shilling immediately, then it must be worth more. So, before she could talk herself out of it, she said, "Three shillings."

The man glared at her, and she felt Ida tug on her hand insistently. She didn't have to look down to know the little girl wanted her to take it back and accept the first deal.

But Ellie maintained eye contact with the man. "Three shillings, sir."

Finally, he let out a scoff that sounded almost like a laugh. "I can give ye two shillings, miss. Not a cent more."

She grinned. "Deal." That was a whole week's pay for her. Even though the pawnbroker chuckled to himself as he gave her the coins, implying Ellie could have haggled for more, she didn't care. Those two shillings were precious to her.

After they left the shop, Ida looked up at her, grinning. "Two shillings!"

"All thanks to you," Ellie said, laughing. She pulled the girl in for a hug.

"What happens now?" Ida asked.

"Now we feast," Ellie said. "Properly."

They went to the market and bought roasted meat and bowls of hot stew. They savoured every bite of it, licking their bowls clean, before buying bread for the next day. They ended up back at their doorstep, their stomachs full for the first time in years.

Ida leaned against Ellie, smiling. "My stomach don't hurt no more," she said. "I forgot this feeling."

Ellie was feeling content and sleepy. "I did, too. I haven't felt like this since my parents. It's wonderful."

"I just wish Daisy and Luke were here to share in the good fortune," Ida whispered.

Ellie smiled, feeling melancholy like she always did when she thought of their lost friends, but it didn't hurt so much now. A full belly really did wonders for the soul. She wrapped an arm around Ida and pulled her close.

"Where do you think Luke is right now?" Ida asked. "He must be still alive. He's gotta be."

"I hope so," Ellie whispered. "Maybe he caused a mutiny and took Captain Rowe's position as leader of the ship."

Ida giggled at the thought. "Or he joined a band of pirates, and he's sailing the seven seas."

They giggled together at the idea. Silently, Ellie sent up a prayer, hoping Luke was still alive and getting on as well as he could. She still thought of him often, remembering the twinkle in his eyes, the way his mouth curved up in a smile. And more times than not, she remembered how he had claimed he was going to marry her someday.

How she wished that someday would come, but she knew better. If she'd learned one thing on the streets it was that things rarely if ever went in her favour. She blew out her breath. She shouldn't be thinking that way. She was alive, wasn't she? She had Ida. And she had a job. Daisy was with God and would never have to be cold or hungry again. She had to concentrate on those things. She reached over and took Ida's hand. Ida gave her a questioning look but then smiled. She seemed to somehow know what Ellie had been thinking.

The next day, work was easier. Ellie felt stronger after having a decent meal the night before and a fat piece of bread for lunch. She got through the day with more energy and felt decently happy for the first time in a long time. She felt a pang of sadness that she couldn't live like this every day. The extra money would already be gone by the time her shift ended because she had given it to Ida to purchase a new bag and two dresses from the rag seller. Ellie had mended their dresses as much as she was capable, with an old needle and thread scraps from the shop, but they were falling apart at the seams and full of holes.

After today, it would be back to conserving food and savouring every bite. That was all right, though. She was grateful for the chance to have a full meal.

"Someone's in a good mood," Amelia said at the end of the day.

Ellie smiled at her. "I'm getting a dress."

"That's wonderful! What colour are you thinking of? I think green would look beautiful on you, or blue."

"I'll take whatever colour is available," Ellie said laughing. "As long as it's decent and is better than threadbare."

Amelia giggled. "So practical. You should find a red dress, if you can. It would look lovely with your scarf."

Ellie looked down at Luke's scarf and smiled. "Perhaps." She touched it softly. Even though she doubted she would ever see

Luke again, she was happy she still had something of his to remember him by.

Ida was waiting for her, just outside the shop. She had a different bag. It was worn and dirty, just like the last one, but there were far fewer holes. She had also changed into a faded blue dress made from worn, slightly stained wool. It hung on her thin frame like a flour sack, but it was a sight better than what she was wearing before.

"I have a dress for you as well," she said. "It's not a lot, but we'll be able to sell your old ones for a penny or two."

She pulled the new dress out of the bag. It was dark green cotton. It was threadbare in a few places and the hem was ragged and in desperate need of repair, but it looked beautiful to Ellie. She took it gingerly in her hands.

"It's perfect. Thank you."

They found the nearest alley out of sight from the main street, and Ida kept watch as Ellie hurried to put on her new dress. It was a little loose on her, but she loved it. She joined Ida on the street again, and they smiled at each other.

Luke would say we look like princesses, all dressed up to go to a ball.

The thought crossed her mind, unexpected and unwanted. Part of her wished she could forget him. Most of her knew she never would.

Ida looked a little sad as well. Was she thinking about Daisy or Luke? Maybe both. Ellie took Ida's hand with hers. "Now that we look like proper ladies, let's go to the market and get ourselves a cup of tea."

Ida nodded eagerly. As they walked to the market, they passed a bakery. The door opened just as they were approaching.

"You two," the baker said, pointing at them.

They froze and stared at him. Ellie pointed at herself hesitantly. "Us?"

He nodded impatiently. "Yes, you two. Come inside. I ain't got all day."

Nervously, Ellie and Ida entered the shop. It was warm inside, and the aroma of bread was heavenly. Ellie's mouth watered, but she couldn't help but be wary.

"Have we done something to offend you, sir?"

She didn't know why else he would single them out and bring them into the shop.

"Of course not," he said, his voice gruff. "I see you two on me way to work, sleepin' on a doorstep. And you," he pointed at Ida, "Go through my rubbish pile at all hours of the day, but you always run off before I can have a word with ye."

Ida hung her head, looking dejected. Ellie also felt ashamed. She no longer felt like a princess. All she was, was a ragamuffin shop girl. "I'm sorry, sir," she said. "We won't bother ya again."

"Bloody right, ya won't." He reached behind his counter and brought out two loaves of bread, in packages. "Cus I'm given' ye my leftover bread outright."

They stared at the bread. *This must be some kind of trick,* Ellie thought to herself.

The baker looked at them with raised eyebrows, and when it was clear neither of them were going to say anything, then he continued. "I would have said something sooner, but this is the first time I've been able to catch ye when ya two weren't sleepin'. I used to live in the slums and remember how people looked down on me and my family, even though we were as hard workin' as any folk. A baker took a chance on me an' offered me an apprenticeship. I told myself I would help someone else if I could. So go on, take the bread. No trick or trap here."

Hesitantly, the two girls took the bread. Ellie tore off a piece of her loaf and savoured the taste of it. It was only slightly stale, and it tasted like heaven.

"Thank you, sir," she said. "Is there anything we can do in return?"

He nodded. "I want to strike a deal with the little one here." He turned to Ida. "If you come in here and help me for a few hours every night, I'll give ye whatever didn't sell. Would rather it go to you two than in the rubbish."

Ida's eyes shone with happiness. "Do you mean it, sir?"

"Of course, I mean it. Don't get too excited. It will be hard work, an' I can't afford to pay ye. But you'll get some food and a few hours inside a warm building for yer trouble."

"Thank you," Ida said, practically jumping up and down with happiness. "I won't let you down, sir. I promise."

He smiled kindly. "I know you won't. Now, let's start tonight. Grab a broom from that side closet over there, and start sweepin' the floor for me." He looked at Ellie. "I'm afraid I only have enough extra work for one helpin' hand. But if I'm not mistaken, you work at the dress shop around the corner, right?"

She nodded. "Yes, sir. Thank you, sir."

He waved his hand dismissively. "If you wanna thank me, then ya can help yer sister tonight."

Ellie nodded. "Yes, sir. Thank you."

Happiness surged through her. Helping the baker meant Ida wouldn't have to scavenge through the rubbish piles anymore, and both would have food every day. That, combined with Ellie's money from the dress shop, would be enough for them to stay fed and take shelter on cold nights. With some careful planning, she would even be able to save a few coins in case one of them got ill or needed medicine.

It'll be okay, she thought to herself. *We'll be able to survive.*

PART III

CHAPTER 9

Four years later

Luke's hands were bleeding from scrubbing the deck of the ship, but at least that meant he couldn't focus on the lash marks on his back. The hot sun burned into him, but he hardly noticed it.

Captain Rowe's footsteps echoed on the deck. *Keep moving,* Luke prayed. *Don't notice me. Keep moving.*

No such luck. The captain stopped right next to him.

"You call this deck clean, you lazy rat? It looks even dirtier than when you started it!" He gave a sharp kick to Luke's side. Pain exploded through him, and he collapsed against the deck, coughing. The captain laughed. "Start over and do it right this time, or I'll toss you overboard."

It was an empty threat, and Luke knew it. The captain paid a pretty penny for Luke, and he would have to pay more to replace him. Besides, the cleanliness of the decks wasn't what really mattered to the captain. He just wanted to punish Luke for sneaking extra food from the galley. At least the captain didn't catch on to the fact that Luke only stole the food to give to an ill crewmate. Then they both would have been punished.

He got more seawater and started to scrub the deck again. As he did so, he let his thoughts wander to more pleasant times. He thought of Daisy and Ida, who were like little sisters to him. He missed their smiles and laughs, and he hoped they were doing well. But most of the time, his thoughts drifted toward Ellie. Thinking of her was as painful as it was sweet.

When he first met her, he saw her as nothing more than someone to keep him company. It was nice having someone to talk to, and he was more than happy to provide protection in exchange for that. But as the years went on, his attachment to her grew. She was so fierce and kind, even when life was cruel to her. No matter how hard things got, she never got nasty or lost her temper. She was always willing to sacrifice food and clothing for the little girls– and for him, when he would let her. She was also beautiful. He reckoned she was the most beautiful girl he'd ever seen.

She had probably forgotten about him. He didn't know how long exactly he'd been on the ship, but he knew years had passed. He was a lot older, covered in scars, and with a thick beard. Every time he caught his reflection during calm seas, or in a piece of polished metal, he hardly recognized himself.

For all Luke knew, Ellie was married to someone, and good for her. She deserved happiness. He just hoped her husband was a good man with a good job who was able to give her the life she deserved. That was something he could never do. Not while he was trapped on this ship.

He finished scrubbing the deck, feeling thoroughly miserable. Rowe passed by him again. "That will do," he said. "No dinner for you. Thieves don't eat on my ship. You'll keep watch tonight. All night."

It looked like Rowe was still punishing him, then. Normally Luke didn't get that much attention from the captain, and he liked it that way. He knew better than to complain.

"Aye, Captain," he said, keeping his gaze down.

Luke climbed the crow's nest to keep watch while everyone else went to the mess hall to eat. Soon, it would only be him, and the helmsman awake tonight. Even though he wouldn't get a chance to sleep tonight, he didn't mind keeping watch. It was peaceful up here at night. Some of the other men found it painfully dull, but not Luke.

At first after he had first been captured, he found the night—quiet except for the lapping of the waves against the water—eerie. It was much different than the constant noise from the city. But over the years, he had grown to like it.

There wasn't much chance of trouble. The weather was calm, and they hadn't seen another ship in days.

Luke let his eyes adjust to the darkness as he sat back and watched. He let the hours drift by as he tortured himself with more thoughts of Ellie. He imagined her with her husband– maybe a baker or another tradesman. He would be a good man, because she wouldn't settle for anything less. Maybe she would take in laundry to help earn some coin, or maybe he earned enough for both of them. Daisy and Ida would still be living with them, naturally. Perhaps Ida was working in a shop. Maybe Daisy got to go to school. She would do well in school. She was smart enough.

He didn't know how long he was lost in thought, but he realized the air was smelling different. He didn't know how to explain it, even to himself, but it was one of the instincts he'd developed after so much time at sea. He could tell by the scent in the air that they were approaching land.

He strained his eyes in the darkness and could see the faint glow of lights and the silhouettes of buildings in the distance. He felt mostly indifferent to the sight of land. He was never allowed off the ship for fear he would escape.

He stared at the approaching land, only a few leagues away, just because it was something to look at. However, the longer he stared, the more he realized he recognized the buildings. Excitement and grief prickled under his skin as he stood up and leaned forward, against the side of the crow's nest. He knew those buildings all right. They were approaching London.

Something about the sight of those buildings awakened feelings of hope and determination inside of him— two emotions he had been careful to bury as much as possible over the years. They were so close to his home, and he knew he would never get another chance like this. A chance to escape and fulfil his promise to Ellie.

Before he could talk himself out of it, he climbed out of the crow's nest, careful to move quietly so the helmsman wouldn't hear. His feet landed on the deck with a soft thud, and he held his breath, listening. If someone caught him away from his post, he would spend the next morning being flogged in front of everyone. Again.

But there was no alarm. He didn't hear footsteps from the helmsman checking on him. With any luck, the man would have fallen asleep at his post.

He crept to the side of the ship and looked down. The water looked far away. It might be the middle of summer, but he also knew the water would be freezing. What he was about to do was incredibly stupid and reckless, but he knew he would never get another chance like this. As soon as daylight hit, the captain would lock Luke below decks, along with any other unpaid sailor aboard the ship, and keep them there until they left London.

He took a deep breath, said a silent prayer, and pitched himself overboard. For a moment, his stomach flip-flopped as he rushed to the water's surface. Then he felt the cold slap of the water, freezing him in place for a moment. *Move!* he shouted at himself. Through pure determination and desperation, he willed himself to move and start swimming.

Distantly he heard running footsteps and shouts, and he knew his escape had been discovered, but he had much more important things to worry about now, like how the waves kept trying to slam his body against the hull of the ship and how the current kept trying to bring him under. He fought against both with all his might, using every scrap of strength in his body, mixed with adrenaline and fear.

He didn't allow himself to think about his stupid, reckless choice, or how agonizing it would be to drown in the ocean. He just kept moving until the current's pull didn't feel so strong. When he looked back, he saw he had put a lot of distance between himself and the ship. He didn't spend a lot of time counting his blessings, however. He kept swimming toward the shore because he knew every second in the water was a second closer to death or to being back home.

He should have waited until they were closer to London before throwing himself overboard. Hours went by and the sun rose high in the sky, and he was still swimming. He knew the ship would have docked by now. But as long as he was alive, he would keep swimming.

His eyes started to drift shut, though and his body felt like it was freezing up. He knew he was fading away. London docks were still far away. He kept his eyes on it, even as his body stopped swimming.

I tried, Ellie. I hope you live a wonderful life.

He thought about how he had traded himself for the girls, all those years ago. He never regretted it, not once. He smiled as he closed his eyes, imagining Ellie talking and laughing with Daisy and Ida.

The next thing he knew, his body was rocking gently with the waves, but he wasn't in the water anymore. Splintering, damp wood cushioned him. At first, he thought he was dead, but the pain radiating through his body told him he was very much alive. His eyes flickered open as he looked up at the blue sky up above.

"Lord help us all!" called a gravelly voice. "'He's awake! John! You hear me?"

"Course I hear you, Sam. The boat ain't that bloody big." A face floated into view. It belonged to an older man, with grey hair and a sun-tanned face. "You're one lucky rascal, you know that?"

Luke opened his mouth, but the man—John, he was sure—waved him off.

"Save your strength," he said. "We'll be on land soon enough, and we'll get you properly dry and warm. If your luck holds, then you'll make it out of this alive."

Luke realized he was no longer wearing his own clothes and was instead covered with a heavy jacket that smelled like fish and tobacco smoke. That was probably the only reason why he was still alive. It also sank in that he was free from Captain Rowe, and thanks to these fishermen, he would be okay. Somehow, he would find a way to thank these two men. After he regained his strength, at least.

He was bone tired and cold. Despite the pain soaking into his muscles, it was easy for him to fall into a deep sleep.

When he next woke, he was on solid land again. There was a lumpy pillow under his head and a blanket had been thrown on top of him. Heat from a fire warmed his face and body and it felt wonderful even though he still felt weak and cold. His teeth chattered a little as he struggled to sit up and look around. He was in a small, one-room flat. There wasn't much to look at except two straw pallets and a fireplace that acted as a kitchen.

"Don't move," said John. The old man came into view, holding some dishes. "I 'ave some hot tea and soup for ye. I suggest you down 'em as quick as you're able."

Luke took the tea from him and sipped it. The hot liquid burned the roof of his mouth, but it also finally warmed his insides. When he finished the tea, he took the soup and drank this much slower, even though he was starving for food. The last thing he wanted was to vomit all over John's floor.

The fisherman watched Luke with speculative eyes. "Word on the docks is that some idiot jumped to his death from the *Northern Star*. I'm not a bettin' man, but I reckon that was you."

Luke nodded, feeling wary.

John sighed. "I ain't gonna tell no one you're alive. The way I see it, it's a miracle you survived your swim, and it took about twenty more miracles to keep you from losin' your fingers and toes. Judgin' from the scars on your back, you had good reason to jump."

Luke swallowed. "Thank you." His voice was hoarse and thick.

He shrugged. "Just glad we made it in time. You can stay here until you get your strength up. All I ask is you're respectful to my brother and me."

"Yes, sir."

"None of that 'sir' crap. The name is John. My brother's Sam. He's out at the dock right now, puttin' in the work of two people. Your name?"

"Luke."

He nodded. "Nice to meet ya, Luke."

"It's nice to meet you as well." Luke swallowed. "Is there any way I can repay ye?"

"Just regain yer strength first. We can talk from there. I assume you're handy on a ship."

"Yes, s-" He had to stop himself at the last minute before calling John 'sir'. At least he hadn't called him Captain. On the *Northern Spirit*, he wasn't allowed to call anyone by their first names, only their titles. The only exception to that rule were the other unpaid deckhands who Rowe purchased for free labour. It would take some time to adjust to being a free man again.

John didn't comment on Luke's mistake. "After you get your strength up, you can help us on our fishing boat for a few days. It won't be easy work, but we'll treat you with more respect than Rowe did."

Luke nodded. "Thank you." Part of him wanted to ask if John could find out anything about Ellie, Daisy, and Ida. But the chances of him being able to find three street urchins in an entire city felt slim. When he was better and had paid his debt to John and Sam, he would find them himself. He didn't care how long it took.

John and Sam were gone for long hours at a time, working their fishing vessel in the early hours of the morning before taking their catch back to the docks to sell to the local markets. Luke wanted to help them almost immediately, but John made him rest for two days.

"Ye ain't doin' us any good if ye pass out on the boat, or if those cuts on your back start festerin'," he said. "Yer stayin' in bed until yer better. We ain't got much, but we can spare a sick man some tea and stew for a couple of days."

Sam agreed. He was a cheerful man, a few years younger than his brother, and he was also happy to have Luke around. "Yer the most excitement we've had in a long time," he said. "Besides, you'll find no affection for Captain Rowe here. We met 'im once at the tavern, and 'e's a right rat. Gettin' one over on him is an absolute delight."

"Thank you," Luke said. "I'm very grateful to both of ya."

Sam waved him off. "No need to thank us. We'll get what we're owed and then some when yer fit for work again."

Luke spent two days in bed, drinking hot soup and tea. He had never had the luxury to truly rest before, especially in a bed. The only other time he took time off like this was when he was confined to that bakery cellar with severe illness. But the brother's home was warm, and the straw pallet was comfortable. He spent two days dozing and thinking about Ellie, except during mealtimes, when he enjoyed having a full belly for the first time in his life.

However, by the end of the second day, he was itching to get back to work. All this leisure time was making him restless. His strength had returned, and his injuries were either mostly or completely healed. So, the next day, he woke up with John and Sam and went with them to their small fishing vessel.

The work was hard, as hard as his work on the *Northern Spirit*. But the brothers were kind and good humoured, so it wasn't long before camaraderie was built between the three of them. John was a little more withdrawn, but he was quick to smile, especially as Sam cracked jokes and talked with Luke. The younger brother was full of questions for Luke, especially his life before Captain Rowe.

Luke was honest. "I was on the streets," he told Sam as they were on their way back to the docks with a successful haul. "I grew up in London. I did beggin', mudlarkin', and the like to get by until I was nineteen or twenty or so."

"I'm surprised a street-smart fellow like ye got caught," Sam said. "If you survived that long, then ye must have known who to steer clear from."

Luke grimaced, remembering that horrible morning. He still remembered it in detail, because he revisited that memory— and all of the fear and anger that came along with it— all too often. "They got me when I was asleep," he said. "I would have fought them off, but I was with a few girls. I told 'em I wouldn't put up much of a fight if the hoodlums let the girls go, and they agreed."

Sam raised his eyebrows. "That's noble of ya."

Luke shrugged. He didn't see it that way. He never would have survived the pain of knowing Ellie was meeting some horrible fate at the hands of a lech, let alone Daisy and Ida, who were still so young. Going with those men and keeping them away from the girls was by far the easier option for himself. "They were my friends, and they looked out for me. The least I could do was look out for them."

"What were their names?" John asked.

"Daisy, Ida... and Ellie." He couldn't help but smile a little as he said her name. It was the first time he had spoken it aloud in five years. Saying it again sent a warm feeling through him, along with a stab of pain and longing. He missed her.

Sam grinned, immediately picking up on the smile. "Ellie, huh? Was she your love?"

He shook his head, smiling. His cheeks grew warm, though. It felt strange to talk about Ellie again, but it also felt good, especially with two men that he trusted.

"We was both too young," he said. "Even if we wasn't, we were too busy lookin' after ourselves and two little ones to be. But I wanted to marry her. Still do." He had daydreamed about marrying Ellie a lot during the early days on the *Northern Spirit*. The thought of her walking down the aisle to meet him had kept him going on even the darkest of days. But as more time passed, he started to lose hope of ever getting his freedom again, let alone making his way back to Ellie, Ida, and Daisy. So, his musings grew darker as he imagined her marrying someone else.

"Have you heard word of her since then?" Sam asked.

"No, not a thing. But there was no way either of us could get word to the other. I was never allowed off the ship, so I never had a way of gettin' a message to her. I had no way of receivin' them, if she wanted to send a message to me. I want to find her, though. Eventually." Now that it was a possibility to find her, the thought made him nervous. What if she wanted nothing to do with him after he had been gone for so long?

John looked at him with a speculative look in his eye. Without knowing it, he gave voice to Luke's fears. "It's been five years," John said. "How do ye know she hasn't found 'erself another fella?"

Luke swallowed as an image of Ellie at the altar flashed through his mind, but this time with an unknown man. Maybe a costermonger, or a baker. It would be good if he were a baker. Then she would never go hungry again.

"I don't know if she's married," he said quietly. "If she 'as, then I'm happy for her. I still want to see her, though. Make sure she's okay. I wanna see Daisy and Ida again too." He smiled, doing his best to put on a brave face. "I'm sure Daisy's doin' well, no matter where she is. She was always small, even for her age, but she 'as a way of keepin' a smile on her face, no matter 'ow bad things get."

It was too easy to imagine her bright smile. No matter how hungry and tired she was, she was always smiling. It was as if she knew her smile cheered up the others and gave them the strength to keep going.

Sam grinned. "I 'ope you find them again," he said. "Who knows? Maybe you an' this Ellie will have a wedding before the year is out."

Luke snorted at the thought, but his chest ached. Even though he was back in London, Ellie seemed just as far away as when he was on Captain Rowe's boat.

On the third day of Luke working with the brothers, John surprised him by giving him a portion of the earnings. "Ye worked for free for two days," he said. "Two days of work in exchange for two days of bedrest. Seems fair, don't it?"

Luke didn't know what to say. He assumed it would be much longer before his debt was paid. Not only that, but this was the first time in five years that he held money in his hand. The dirty coins felt like a small fortune to him even though it was worth barely more than a cup of tea and a meat pie at the market.

John gave him a small smile, as if he understood Luke couldn't figure out how to form an answer. He clapped the young man on the shoulder.

"Most of the earnin's go to takin' care of the boat and our equipment, but you'll get an equal share of the rest. Ye can stay with us too, as long as you pitch in with the rent and take yer turn cleanin' and cookin'."

"I..." Again, Luke's words failed him. How was he supposed to respond to this man's kindness? He hadn't known a lot of kindness in his life, apart from Ellie, Daisy, and Ida. If John told him he would be working for free for the next year in exchange for pulling him out of the water, then Luke wouldn't have questioned it. He would have considered himself lucky. But now the older brother was declaring him a free man after only two days. How was that enough to repay them for all the trouble of saving him and feeding him?

Sam chuckled. "Don' look so shocked. We were already thinkin' of gettin' a third fishermen on our boat, and ye saved us the trouble of findin' someone who could pull his weight without causin' a fuss. You ain't so bad. It 'elps that yer pleasant company to be around. We could 'ave ended up stuck on the boat for hours a day with a right scoundrel."

"Thank you," Luke finally managed, looking at the two brothers.

John shook his head, and Luke expected him to get admonished for thanking them again, but the older man just said, "Tis no trouble." He gave him a small smile, and Luke knew he was secretly really pleased.

A month went by, and Luke worked hard to make sure he was useful to the brothers. Not only was he handy on the ship, but he had a knack for repairing their equipment and keeping it in good shape. His earnings mostly went to rent and food, but he was able to save a few pennies here and there. After buying a straw pallet and some new clothes and a coat for winter, Luke didn't have anything to spend his money on, so he kept the extra coins in a sock, hidden under his mattress. Just having extra coins to hang onto instead of immediately spending on food made him feel like he was living like a king.

Sometimes, when the brothers would go to a nearby tavern for some drinks, Luke would walk along the wharf. When the taverns were open, there weren't a lot of people hanging out outside, so it was nice and peaceful.

He liked to walk down to an abandoned building that was off to the side. Not a lot of people went near it and there were even some rumours that it was haunted. The roof was falling apart, and the door was hanging off one hinge, so the building had seen better days. But it was the sort of building that he, Ellie, Daisy, and Ida would seek out when they needed some shelter for the night. He could not help but stare at the building sometimes, feeling intrigued by it. He did not know what he wanted to do with the place, but he couldn't stop thinking about the growing number of coins he possessed and wondered if he could one day buy a building like that and fix it up to be habitable.

Autumn came quickly and the harsh wind from the ocean chilled Luke to the bone, even with his new jacket. But he didn't let himself get slowed down at work. Instead, he worked even faster, hoping to keep the blood moving. But at the end of the day, his toes were numb with a cold that reminded him a little too much of his frantic swim in the ocean, away from Captain Rowe's ship.

One windy evening, he couldn't help a sigh of relief and be grateful that the day was finally over, and he could collapse on his straw pallet and rub his hands together for warmth while Sam cooked stew over the coal stove. He took his boots and socks off so he could rub heat into his toes as well as his hands.

John gave him his share of the earnings, and Luke was quick to put the coins with the others in the old sock, which now carried some weight and jingled around. The older man watched him with a thoughtful look. "What ya savin' those for?"

Luke shrugged. A vision of the abandoned building on the wharf flashed through his mind, but he couldn't bring himself to say it. The thought of buying the building seemed too foolish to say out loud. "Don' know. Rainy day, maybe. Better to 'old onto them while I can."

The older brother settled down on his own pallet and gave Luke a speculative look. "At least ye don' waste yer coin on drink."

Luke grimaced and shook his head. "I had it once on the ship, and it made me feel funny and throw up. I'll take tea over alcohol any day of the week."

Sam chuckled. "A sailor without a taste for liquor? I never thought I would see the day."

"It's profitable for ya," John said, nodding to the coin sock. "Ye know, if you keep savin' those, then you could start yer own business if you want. Ya could get your own ship."

Luke snorted. "I could have a century to hoard coins and still not have enough to buy even a dinghy."

Sam started to dish the food into bowls. "What about settin' up shop, repairin' fishing gear? Yer mighty fine at that. It'll give ye enough to settle down with yer girl."

Luke felt a pang in his chest at the thought of Ellie. Now and then he regretted telling Sam and John about her. He felt strangely vulnerable at the thought of them knowing about her.

"She's not my girl," he said, looking at the dingy wall instead of at either of the brothers. "It's been five years. She's probably forgotten about me and married someone else. Besides, I wouldn't even know how to find her."

Nothing short of bad weather gave them a day off from fishing, so even if Luke had some clue where Ellie was, he wouldn't have the time to find her. He had to admit this was probably an excuse instead of a reason. The truth was, he was scared to find her and find out he was no longer welcome in her life.

But the brothers weren't having it.

"Ye can take the day off tomorrow," John said as Sam handed

him his bowl of stew. "Go find her. Ye'll never know if she's married unless you go."

Luke frowned, hoping to cover up his trepidation. "What about you two?"

"We've gotten on long enough by ourselves," John said. "Besides, this girl is obviously important to ye."

Sam handed Luke a bowl of stew. "Ye should find 'er. Then ye can either have a beautiful reunion and marry 'er, or ye can move on and find someone else."

Luke was tempted to ask why they cared about if he married or not, when neither brother had ever married, as far as he knew.

"Have either of ye married?"

The two men paused and looked at each other before looking at Luke.

"No," John said. He busied himself on eating the stew. "There was a girl I fancied once. She was the prettiest thing I ever did see. But she never 'ad eyes for me, and she ended up marryin' someone else. I don't know what happened to her." He frowned slightly before taking a sip of his soup. "Never had the time to find someone else. When I'm not workin', I'm either drinkin' to forget a bad day, or I'm restin' up for the next one. No time for me to court someone properly. Besides, I can 'ardly bring a gal 'ere, with this one in the way."

Sam made an indignant sound. "That's big talk from someone with a bowl full of stew in 'is hands, made by yers truly."

"It's burnt and bland, like usual." John grunted. "Sometimes I think you muck it up on purpose because yer hopin' to be relieved of cooking duty. Fat bloody chance of that."

"I beg your pardon, but I'm an excellent cook."

"Luke makes better food than you, and the kid grew up starvin' on the streets."

Luke grinned, feeling himself relax as the brothers eased into the familiar bickering. He was tempted to let them all fall into the easy routine again, but he couldn't help but be curious about Sam.

"Did you ever 'ave a girl, Sam?"

"Oh, there were none that ever caught my eye," he said. "Plenty went after me. I was always the 'andsome one in the family."

John let out a sound that sounded like a cross between a snort and a laugh, but Sam ignored him.

"But if I'm bein' honest, I never wanted a kid of me own. I remember watchin' our parents struggle to feed us and take care of us. We had two other brothers, ye know. But they both died of fever before we reached our teen years. Our mum never recovered from it, not really." The younger brother grimaced at the memory, and John looked more sombre than usual. "I knew I could watch a child die if I married, so I knew I would need to find someone truly special if I was goin' to risk that. I never found anyone worth that risk." He shrugged. "Such is life, I guess."

Luke understood what he was saying. The thought of losing a child was excruciating. He had never considered the possibility of having children and being a father. It already felt fantastical imagining Ellie would marry him, especially when they had been apart for so long. But he knew, despite Sam's words, he would marry Ellie in a heartbeat if she agreed to it. Ellie was worth the risk.

However, if she wouldn't have him, then he knew he would never marry. He would never find someone as special as Ellie again, and he would rather be a bachelor, living in the flat with the two brothers for the rest of his days before settling for someone else.

He sipped his stew as he mulled over everything the brothers had told him. The thought of going after Ellie was pleasant, but it also sent a thrill of fear down his back. What if she had forgotten about him or wanted nothing to do with him after all these years? Even worse, what if something had happened to her because he wasn't there to stop it? He would never forgive himself for that. But he also knew the brothers were right. If he didn't go find Ellie, and at least talk to her, then he would always be wondering about her, and he would never move on. He had to at least try to find her.

The next day, while Sam and John went to work, Luke left the docks and went into the city for the first time since escaping Captain Rowe's ship. It was strange being back in his old territory. Very little had changed since he left, but now and then he saw a new storefront, or an old building with a freshly painted sign out front, and he was reminded that he had been gone for half a decade.

He walked around, feeling a little lost as to where to begin searching for them. For all he knew, the three girls had moved on from this part of London long ago, and there was a good chance his search would be fruitless. Even worse was the possibility he found out something horrible had happened to them. Maybe all three of them were in paupers' graves, or maybe they got snatched at some point in the last five years and were now lost to him and enduring some horrible fate. But he needed to look anyway. He needed to at least try to find them.

He went to the markets, looking for any sign of Ellie with a street seller's tray and a supply of matches to sell, but there was no sign. He asked a few of the sellers about her, but no one knew who he was talking about. No one recognized the descriptions he gave of Ida and Daisy either.

He checked the riverbank of the Thames, in case Daisy and Ida were mudlarking. Even though he saw plenty of children scavenging along the banks, none of them looked like the two little girls he had protected for so many years.

The streets were getting darker as night began to fall. Luke bought himself a meat pie as he walked, feeling a wave of nostalgia from eating a meat pie in this part of London. The only difference was, he was able to buy it easily instead of stealing it when the seller's back was turned.

He was starting to feel discouraged, but he wasn't ready to give up for the night just yet. As he walked down the street, he was debating checking the penny sit up shelters to see if there were any sign of the girls, or if he should just give up and go back home when he heard her.

Even though she wasn't talking any louder than anyone else in the crowded London streets, he was able to pick out her voice in the crowd as easily as he could five years ago.

Ellie.

Her voice was more subdued than he remembered, and it sounded older, but it was her. He broke into a run, following the sound around the corner, to a clothing factory. He stopped short when he saw her.

She was older, of course, but no less beautiful. Her brown hair was pinned up into a bun, but after a long day at work, sections of her hair had fallen out to frame her face. She wore a dark blue dress that was bordering on threadbare, but it was clean. Around her neck was the red scarf he had given her all those years ago. It was a little faded, but the sight of it filled him with hope. If she still wore that scarf, then maybe she had not forgotten about him. Maybe she still cared about him the same way he cared about her. Despite the exhaustion on her face, she looked healthier than the last time he saw her. At least, she looked like she wasn't on the brink of starvation.

He didn't recognize the girl she was with until she turned slightly in his direction. *Ida.* Exhaustion lined her face as well, and even though she was smiling—it didn't reach her eyes, at least not in the same way he remembered. Where was Daisy?

He walked up to them, feeling like he was in a daze. Even as he kept his eyes fixed on Ellie, he couldn't help but wonder if this was some sort of hallucination brought on by wishing too hard. Maybe he was about to approach two strangers who happened to look like his friends. If so, then he would never live that down. As he approached, they turned to look at him. The wariness on their faces turned to recognition and then shock.

"L-Luke?" Ellie whispered, as if she scarcely dared to believe it.

"Ellie," he said, relief filling him. It was really her standing before him. After so many years, they were finally together again. Her face crumpled, and she let out a sob before running toward him and throwing her arms around him in a hug.

He hugged her back and closed his eyes, savouring the feeling of her in his arms again. He felt a lump form in his own throat. He looked at Ida, who was still staring at him as if he was a mirage. He gave her a soft, crooked smile as he held out his arm to her. She ran up and gave him a hug as well.

They stayed like that for several minutes before pulling back. As they did so, he couldn't help but ask. "Where is Daisy?"

Ida and Ellie looked like they were about to cry again. That was when Luke noted Ida's jacket. It was the same jacket he had given Daisy all those years ago. There would be only one reason why Ida would be wearing the jacket instead of Daisy. Only one reason why Daisy wasn't here with them.

"No," he whispered, his voice breaking. "Not Daisy." He could still picture her smiling face so easily. She was always so happy, and so brave. He couldn't believe…

But the look on their faces confirmed his worst fears. Ellie grabbed his hand. "Come on. We have much to tell each other."

CHAPTER 10

Ellie could scarcely believe Luke was here, in front of her. He looked older. His face was tanned from days of being out in the sun on the open sea, and there were scars visible on his face and hands. But he was just as handsome as she remembered. She couldn't help but wonder what he thought, seeing her again after all these years.

The three of them found a bench that was not far from the bakery. They all sat down together. Luke's face was tight with grief.

"When did it happen?" he asked.

"Four years ago," Ellie told him. Pain stabbed at her heart as she thought of Daisy again and that horrible day. "Sh-she got sick with fever. I tried to buy her medicine, but we didn't have the money. So, we tried to keep her clean and to feed her."

Ida took a deep breath, and Ellie knew she was holding back a sob. "We 'oped she would get better the way you did," she said. Her voice cracked on the last word. She bit her lip and shook her head rapidly, unable to voice what happened next.

Luke sucked in his breath before pulling the two girls into a hug. "I'm so sorry," he said. "I should have been there. I should have…" his voice trailed off.

"I'm just glad you came back," Ida said. "The last we 'eard, you was on the *Northern Spirit* with Captain Rowe. We kept goin' to the docks for a while, but there was never any sign of you."

"It took me a long time to escape," he whispered. "Captain Rowe, he… he's a mean old man. I can tell ya that much. He kept me and any other unpaid crew members locked up below deck every time we reached land. It was only by chance and luck I was able to escape when I did. A month ago, he was makin' me keep watch at night, when we were approachin' London. I saw the city, and I knew it was my only chance to come home. So, I pitched myself over the edge of the boat."

Ellie gasped. "Luke, you could 'ave been killed!"

"I nearly was," he confessed. "I swam for all I was worth toward the shore, but I felt myself fadin'. Then two brothers in a fishin' boat pulled me out and took me to shore."

He gave them a soft, crooked smile. "Sam and John nursed me back to health, and now I help them on their boat. They're decent fellows. They give me a place to live, food, and a share of the earnin's, so I can't complain." He looked from Ellie to Ida and then back again. "What about you two? The two of you look a mite healthier than when I last saw ye."

Ida smiled. "Ellie got 'erself a job sewing clothes. She works long hours but it's steady pay."

"Did ya now?" Luke smiled at her. The pride was evident on his face, and it made her blush furiously.

"Yes," she mumbled. "I now get three shillings a week for my work. It's not a lot, but it's given us a small measure of comfort and security. But what really 'elps is Ida's job."

Luke's gaze turned to the younger girl. "What's your job, then?"

"I 'elp the baker," she said proudly. "I 'elp clean the bakery at the end of every day while he starts preparin' for the next day. In return, he gives me stale bread that he was goin' to toss in the bin. I get at least two loaves of bread every day."

Luke grinned. "Two loaves of bread a day? How about that? No wonder the two of you are lookin' as healthy as princesses these days. I'm proud of ya. Both of ya."

Ida beamed from the praise, and Ellie felt herself flush with happiness. She had forgotten how good Luke could make her feel with only a few words.

Unfortunately, after only a few more minutes of conversation, Ida reluctantly went to work. But she hugged Luke before she left. "Promise me you'll visit us again," she said. "Sometime soon."

"I'll certainly try," he said as he hugged her back. "Work on the fishin' boat means long hours. But they gave me the day off to find you. I'll come back as soon as I'm able."

Ida waved goodbye as she left, a smile on her face and tears in her eyes.

After she went to the bakery, Ellie and Luke were alone together. She smiled up at him. "Come on. There's a doorstep around the corner that's usually empty. We shouldn't be disturbed."

Together, the two of them walked to the doorstep and sat down together. It felt surreal to have Luke sitting next to her again. It almost felt as if no time had passed at all. At the same time, it felt like an eternity had passed.

"Is this where you two sleep at night?" He asked.

She shook her head. "Not anymore. Between the two of us, we can afford the twopenny hangover most nights. It's warmer, and a little more comfortable."

The shelter also offered bunks for four pennies a night, but neither of them could bear sleeping in those little coffin-like beds, all squished together. It reminded Ellie too much of her parents, and it reminded both her and Ida of Daisy in her pauper's grave. She didn't care if she had to sleep sitting on an uncomfortable bed and hanging over a rope. She wasn't lying down in a coffin. Not until she was well and truly dead.

"Most nights, Ida gets even more than two loaves from the bakery for a few hours of work, so we don't go 'ungry anymore. Sometimes she finds odd jobs during the day for a penny or two. We're savin' up for her to be a street seller when she can't find extra work."

It wouldn't be long until she had enough money to start street selling. The only reason why she wasn't selling matches or flowers already was because Ellie insisted on keeping a few shillings in reserve in case of emergency. Ida didn't argue, not when she knew those shillings could mean life or death if one of them were to fall ill.

"I'm glad to 'ear it," he said, grinning. "I missed ya, Ellie."

She smiled, but she felt her smile tremble a little. "I missed ya too, Luke. I was beginning to think ya weren't comin' back."

"I thought so too," he admitted. "Even after I was free and back in London, I didn't think I'd be able to find ya. But I never stopped thinkin about ya, and hopin' ya was okay."

He reached out to grab her hands. His were still so warm compared to her own.

"I'm sorry I couldn't come back earlier. I'm sorry it took me a month of bein' free before I went searching for ya."

She shook her head. "If yer sorry about that, then I should be sorry for not comin' to the docks no more. Ya didn't know if ya could even find us, and ya needed to keep yer work. I don't blame ya for that."

She remembered all too well the constant aching of hunger and the difficulty of scraping together coins when living on the street. Even now, she and Ida were by no means comfortable. They never seemed to get enough sleep, and their bodies constantly ached from the work and sleeping by leaning over a rope. But it was practically a luxury compared to constantly being in danger of starving or freezing to death on the streets.

Luke was always willing to sacrifice himself to make sure the rest of them had food. She was glad he decided to hold onto steady work that kept him safe and with a full belly instead of risking starvation just for the chance to see them again.

"I still want to give ya the life you deserve," he said. "And Ida too. I want to give ya a home."

She smiled. *It doesn't matter if we have a roof over our heads or not. You were always my home.* But she didn't want to admit that to him. It somehow felt too vulnerable, even with Luke. "We get by just fine, Luke. Maybe it's time to take care of yerself."

"I'm serious, Ellie. Ya can't be goin' to two-penny hangovers forever. Don't ya want your own place? Even if it's in the slums?"

She looked down. "It's not possible," she whispered. "Even if Ida and I could scrape together enough money, no one would ever rent to two women. At least, not at prices we could afford."

"I can get my own place, and ya can stay with me," he said. "I've talked about it with Sam and John, and they think I can set up a business on the docks, repairin' fishin' equipment for folks. I would be able to earn enough to get a place for the three of us. There's even a building I have in mind for the shop. No more sleeping on a rope. The both of ya will have your own beds. You'll have a home, where ya can prepare food and take in laundry instead of goin' to a factory all day. And Ida can stay with us until she settles down with a husband. Doesn't that sound nice?"

Her heart ached at the thought of it. She had wanted to be with Luke for so long, with their own flat together in the slums. But it felt too good to be true. Something would go wrong. As wonderful as this reunion was, it had been so long since she had seen Luke. Maybe one or both had changed too much, and they wouldn't like each other if they lived together. She couldn't bear it to watch him slowly grow disillusioned with her when he realized the woman she had become wasn't the girl he had been thinking of for five long years on that boat.

Did she even deserve happiness? She'd let Daisy die, after all. She'd let him get kidnapped in the first place.

A stabbing pain filled her chest, and she stood up, crossing her arms in front of herself. "You should get home," she said. "It's getting late, and I must hurry. The shelters will be closing their doors soon."

Surprise and hurt flickered over his face. "Did I say somethin' wrong?"

She shook her head. "No. But it's late, and I need to sleep." She started backing away from him, as if he was a danger. Luke would never hurt her, of course. But the safety he was promising somehow seemed just as scary.

He stared at her, without moving as she stepped away. He looked so stricken, that she knew she needed to reassure him. She managed a shaky smile.

"Please visit again soon, when ya can. Perhaps Ida and I can find ya on Sunday. That's my day off." She turned and ran away from him toward the shelter.

She breathed a sigh of relief as she got inside the shelter, just before the doors closed for the night. The attendant on guard glared at her for arriving so late, but he accepted her money and directed her to the benches. She saw Ida on one of the benches. She must have just gotten inside herself. Some nights, Ida worked too late and had to spend the night on the doorstep, but she usually got into the shelter in time.

Ida looked up at her, eyes shining with happiness and looking like she wanted to talk, but there was no talking allowed. Ellie merely grabbed her hand and squeezed it as the rope was placed across them on the benches. As soon as it was tied securely, they leaned over it and tried to get some sleep for the night.

Even though Ellie knew she had another long day of work ahead of her, and every minute of sleep was precious, she had difficulty falling asleep for the night. All she could think about was Luke and seeing him again. Her heart twisted at the horrible look on his face as she left him alone for the night. She hated hurting him like that. But how could she accept what he was saying? How could she dare to believe in a better life? She was lucky just to have some money at the end of the week to share with Ida, just like she was lucky Ida could give her some stale bread every day.

Eventually, Ellie managed to doze before she was woken suddenly by the attendant cutting the rope at six in the morning. She and Ida both jolted awake, along with everyone else on their row. They stood up and stretched, shaking the sleep from their bodies before leaving the shelter.

Once they were outside, Ida gave her part of a stale loaf of bread, which Ellie put in her dress pocket for her lunch.

"Luke is back," Ida said, smiling. "I can't believe it. He's alive and okay and..." She trailed off, looking overwhelmed with happiness. With that joyful expression on her face, Ida looked remarkably like Daisy, and the thought made Ellie's heart twist.

"He'll visit us again," Ellie said. "And perhaps next time, the two of ya can talk properly. He wants to make money by repairing fishing equipment and get his own flat so we could live with him."

"Oh, that would be wonderful," Ida said, twirling around in excitement. "Imagine that! We could sleep in beds instead of over a rope. We could have a fireplace. Wouldn't that be wonderful?"

Ellie regretted saying it. She didn't want Ida to get her hopes up. "It will be a long time before that happens," she said. "If it happens at all. You know how difficult it is to set up shop like that. We barely got you enough money for a seller's tray, let alone your supply of matches to sell."

"But it's Luke. Luke has a way of doing the impossible. He'll give us a real home. I just know it."

Ellie wished she could be as optimistic as she was. But Ida was right. Luke did have a way of doing the impossible. He escaped Captain Rowe, after all. He fulfilled his promise of returning. But how many miracles could someone accomplish in one life?

Even if he did do it, she wasn't sure if she could go through with it. He could provide a good home for Ida, of course, and she would be happy about that. But she wasn't so sure if she could bear to be so close to him and know she would never deserve him. She couldn't truly have him, could she? Maybe one day in the past, he said he would marry her. But that was so long ago. He didn't say anything about marriage this time. He just said he would provide her with a home.

Ellie was lost in her thoughts as she said goodbye to Ida for the day and headed to the shop. She barely noticed as she sat down at her sewing station and started her work. It wasn't long before she got lost in the act of sewing. The nice thing about the weather cooling down was that she didn't sweat so much inside the building, which was always too stuffy and hot in the summer.

At lunch time, she stood up and stretched and rubbed her hands. They always got stiff and numb after so many hours of sewing. Amelia walked over to her with her own lunch of bread and cheese. "How are you?" she asked.

Ellie began eating her piece of bread. "Remember that boy I told you about? The one who was taken all those years ago?"

She nodded. "Of course."

"He's back."

Her eyes widened. "He came back? Are you sure it's him?"

Ellie nodded. "I talked to 'im and everything. It's so wonderful."

Her friend's brow furrowed. "You don't look too 'appy about it."

Ellie bit her lip. "It just feels too good to be true. That's all.

What if we don't get along so good anymore? So much has changed."

"You never know unless you keep talkin' to him. I know no other fella has turned your head for as long as I've known you. If this man is as good as you say he is, then you should give 'im a chance. Good men are rare, you know."

Ellie knew that. She doubted she would find another man as good and noble as Luke for the rest of her life. But it still felt too good to be true.

After work, she met up with Ida like usual, where they could talk for a few minutes and share a cup of tea in the market before Ida went to help the baker.

"Do you think Luke will visit us soon?" Ida asked.

"We'll see. It might be a little bit before he can get away from work again. But we'll go down to the docks on Sunday and find 'im."

Ida grinned. "I can't wait."

Ellie walked Ida to the bakery. The kind baker inside, Mr. Jones, waved cheerfully at Ellie from the window, and she smiled in return before walking on her way through London.

She sat down on a bench and dug into her pocket for the rest of her bread, which was barely more than a bite. She ate it slowly, savouring it, even though it was stale. She knew, for as long as she lived, she would never take bread for granted.

"Ellie."

Luke's voice startled her. He stood only a short distance away from her, his silhouette illuminated by a nearby streetlamp.

"Luke! What are you doing here?"

He sat down on the bench next to her. Today, she could tell he smelled like the ocean. "I wanted to see ya again," he said. "So, I decided to take a walk after work."

"Ya must be tired."

" 's all right," he said, shrugging. "I... I wasn't sure if ye wanted to see me again." He looked at her cautiously. "Ya almost looked scared of me. I just don't know why."

"I ain't scared of ya," she said. "I... forgive me. I can't explain it."

"Ya ain't done anythin' wrong. I was just confused, is all. I still want to provide you with a home, ya know. I want to marry ya."

She squeezed her eyes shut. "Ya can't, Luke. It's been so long. I ain't the same girl you knew before. I know you're just tryin' to make good on your promise from all that time ago, but it don't matter. We were just kids."

"Are you saying you don't want me? Ellie, you're all I've thought about for five years. The thought of marryin' ya kept me alive on the darkest of days. I'm sorry I didn't come sooner, truly. I wanted to, but I wasn't even allowed to know what port we were sailin' into, and I was locked below decks every time we reached land. I tried to escape a few times at first but..." he stopped talking and looked down, a muscle twitching in his jaw.

Ellie couldn't help but reach out to grab his hand. She knew whatever he went through must have been horrid. "I don't blame ya, Luke. Honest. But I don't want to think about marriage and a flat of our own. I don't want to think of good things that will never happen. I just want to enjoy my life now."

He squeezed her hand. "Why couldn't it happen? If ya don't love me, then tell me. I won't say anythin' more about it. I swear."

But she couldn't get those words out. She *did* love him with all her heart. Nothing would change that. Distance and time meant nothing compared to what Luke meant to her, and everything he gave her. A tear fell down her cheek.

He pursed his lips slightly as he gently wiped her tear away. "It's all right, Ellie. I don't wanna upset ya. It don't matter anyway, not yet. Let me save up for the repair shop, and a flat of me own. You'll see. I'll be able to give ya the life you deserve. It will just take some time."

"You don't have to worry about promises you made years ago," she said. "Ya came back, and that's the most important thing. I couldn't have asked for anything more than that."

He looked sad as he brushed a piece of her hair out of her face and tucked it behind her ear. "It's not enough, Ellie," he whispered. "Not enough for me. I promised to give ya the life ya deserved, and that's exactly what I'm gonna do."

Days went by. Sometimes, Luke would come see her at night, after she got out of work. On Sundays, she and Ida would go down to the docks and find Luke after his work was over. They met Sam and John, the two brothers who had taken him in.

Sam grinned at her when he saw her. "So, this is the li'le lady," he said, giving her an exaggerated bow in greeting. "Our Luke is positively smitten with ya, and I can see why."

Ellie blushed and looked down. Ida, standing next to her, laughed. "She's just as smitten with him. Always has been."

She had to resist the urge to elbow Ida gently in the ribs.

Sam chuckled. "Is that so? Well, maybe there really will be a wedding in the future. At least, that's what Luke is hopin' for."

Luke shoved his friend in the shoulder, hard enough to make him lose his balance. Sam laughed.

The older brother, John, looked at them all with a stern look, but there was a hint of laughter in his eyes. "Enough tomfoolery from the lot of ya. Invite the ladies home for supper, like gentlemen."

"Come on," Luke said. "John is cooking tonight. He's a much better cook than Sam. I'll never subject ya to his cookin'."

Sam gave a mock indignant sound as the group walked to their little flat in the slums. All of them had a bowl of stew each, and a cup of weak tea. The flat was warm and cozy, as everyone made conversation. Ellie couldn't help but admire Ida, who was laughing and talking with the rest of them. Luke's reappearance in their lives had breathed new life in her. She was also struck by how grown-up Ida was now. She was almost eighteen. It felt like yesterday that Ellie found the six-year-old girl hiding in the shadows with her little sister. Where had the time gone?

After supper, Luke walked Ida and Ellie to the nearest two-penny hangover. It wasn't the usual one they went to, but it was the only one close enough for them to get to in time, before the doors closed.

"Will ye be okay here tonight?" he asked.

Ellie nodded. "As long as I run fast tomorrow, I'll get to work on time. Thank ya for supper, and the company."

He smiled wistfully at her. "I'm more than happy to give ya that." He took her hand and kissed it lightly. It was barely more than a brush of his lips on her skin, but it made her cheeks grow hot with embarrassment.

Luke hugged Ida goodnight before he left to go back home. Ida smiled up at Ellie. "You two will make a pretty couple," she said. "I've 'eard they marry you for only a couple of pennies on Christmas."

Ellie shook her head, feeling herself blush warmly. "Let's get inside before the doors close for the night."

Despite the teasing from Ida and Sam, Ellie was sure she was safe from having to really have the painful discussion with Luke because they wouldn't even be able to discuss marriage until he managed to get his fishing repair business off the ground. That would take a long time. At least, that was what she thought.

Ida and Ellie spent Christmas with John, Sam, and Luke. As they were eating dinner, Luke brought up the possibility of securing a space for his business. "There's a small building by the wharf," he said. "It's a little rundown, but it's for sale cheap. I'm gonna make an offer on it in a month or two."

Ellie looked at him, surprised and a little nervous. "How do you know it will still be for sale?"

Sam laughed. "No one wants it. It's practically fallin' apart, and it's probably haunted."

"It ain't haunted," John said as he cut into his meat. "No such things as ghosts."

"Don't go tellin' that to any of the sailors," Luke said with a wry grin.

John grunted. "Foolish superstition, if ye ask me. But that place is a death trap. You'll end up 'aunting it yourself if you ain't careful."

"Then you should wait," Ellie said quickly. "You'll find somewhere else. Someplace that ain't gonna kill ya."

"It won't kill me," he said. "It's no worse than that bakery we lived in for a while."

She bit her lip. "You'll have to fix it up, though. No one's gonna wanna do business in a place like that."

"Is true," he said. "And it'll take time and probably a little bit of barterin' and spendin', but I can do it. I can fix it up good."

"This is wonderful, Luke," Ida said, grinning. "Ellie, don't you think this is wonderful news?"

"Yes," she said hesitantly. "Of course. But…" she looked at the brothers. "Doncha need him on the boat?"

"We always knew he'd move on," John said. "Don't get me wrong. He's a good worker, and we'll be sorry to lose 'im. But we want the best for him. He don't want to be a fisherman forever."

Ellie felt her stomach tied up in knots, and she did what she could to avoid Luke's gaze. She knew that as soon as he was settled into his new life as a repairman with his own business, he would start talkin' about marriage again, and she wasn't sure she was ready for that.

Less than two weeks later, she had another surprise. Ida practically ran up to her, grinning, as Ellie was about to enter the shelter for the night. She grabbed Ellie by the elbow and pulled her out of line.

"What are ya doing?" Ellie asked. "We need to go inside, or we won't get a spot."

The shelter was unusually crowded tonight. Perhaps it was because it was a cold January night, with bitter winds and the threat of sleet in the air. If they waited too long, then the shelter would be completely full, and they wouldn't be allowed inside, no matter how much money they were willing to pay.

"Mr. Jones told me the most wonderful thing today," Ida said, her voice breathless from running. "His Aunt Charlotte is a spinster who lives on Byron Street. She's lookin' for someone to live with her to 'elp with the rent and the errands. He told her about me, and today she came into the shop when I was cleanin', and we talked. She wants me to live with her, Ellie!"

Ellie's eyes widened. "Truly?"

Ida nodded, her eyes shining. "I would have my own room and everything. She said I can move in at the end of the week."

"That's wonderful. I'm so happy for you, Ida." She pulled her into a hug, feeling incredibly happy for her. "Maybe she'll teach ya spinning. Then you can always do that if you ever want to give up bein' a street seller."

A little over a month ago, they finally saved enough money to purchase a street seller's tray and plenty of wares for Ida. Instead of matches, she now sold produce and flowers with more success than Ellie ever saw with it. After one lucrative day, Ida confided that she just thought about what Daisy would do if she was a street seller, and how she would charm everyone with her smile and her mannerisms, and she tried to do the same. It made her feel closer to her sister, as well.

"Spinnin' yarn sounds wonderful," Ida said dreamily. "Havin' my own bedroom sounds wonderful too. What would I even do with all that space? And a bed. I can sleep on a bed instead of a rope."

Ellie grinned. "You'll be livin' like a princess."

Ida giggled. "You know what this means, don't you?"

Ellie frowned and shook her head. "What does it mean?"

"It means you can marry Luke. You don't have to worry about me no more. I couldn't go do this unless I knew ya was all right. That ya had someplace of yer own, too. I ain't going if I don't know that."

Ellie bit her lip and looked down. "I-I don't know."

"El-lie!" Ida grabbed Ellie's hands to make her look at her. "You can't be livin' on the streets by yourself. Besides, you know Luke is in love with ya, just like you're in love with him. Ya have to marry him."

Ellie pulled away from Ida and crossed her arm over herself. "Livin' on the streets ain't so bad. I don't even remember what it's like to 'ave a proper home."

Ida's brow furrowed. "You would rather be sleepin' at twopenny hangovers instead of marryin' with Luke? Why? Doncha love him?"

Tears welled up in Ellie's eyes as she thought about Luke, who was always so generous and brave and incredibly handsome. He could have any girl he wanted, if he tried. Why would he want her so badly?

"I don't deserve 'im, Ida. I don't deserve the life he wants to give me, and I'm scared 'e'll realize that and grow to 'ate me. I don't think I could bear it if he did."

"What do ya mean?" Ida asked, looking bewildered. "Of course you deserve him. I've never met two more wonderful people. Of course, you two deserve each other. And ya especially deserve to be happy. I haven't forgotten how ya saved me and Daisy. I won't never forget that."

A lump rose in Ellie's throat at the thought. But she slowly shook her head. "I let Daisy die." Her voice was hoarse and scratchy. "And I couldn't stop 'im from bein' kidnapped. And I couldn't stop Daisy from sufferin'. If I was better, I could have gotten the medicine for her. Or I could have kept her from gettin' sick in the first place. I didn't look after her. Not in the way I should have."

Ida shook her head. "No. What happened with Daisy ain't your fault. She... she just fell ill." Her voice cracked, and she took a deep breath before continuing. "It's not your fault, Ellie. I don't blame ya. And Daisy wouldn't either." She gave her a shaky smile. "You've spent your whole life takin' care of me and Daisy. You deserve to have somethin' for yourself. You deserve to be happy."

Ellie bit her lip. "I don' feel like I do."

"Well, too bad. You do. And he'll tell you the same thing. He's madly in love with ya. He always has been." Ida glanced at the line of people entering the shelter and winced. "As much as I would like to continue to talk, we should get inside before it truly does become too late to get inside."

The two women rushed to join the line, and they were the last people allowed in the shelter for the night. Ellie breathed a sigh of relief once they were inside, and she savoured the moderate amount of warmth from the building.

As they leaned over the rope for the night, Ellie thought about what Ida said. Did Ellie really deserve a chance at happiness? It didn't feel possible. She hadn't done anything so special. All she did was try to keep her family alive, and she couldn't even do that. But Ida was adamant that she deserved happiness. Maybe, just maybe, she could let herself marry Luke. Maybe it would be okay for her to be happy and think of herself, especially when Ida was going to be nice and comfy in a flat with Mr. Jones's aunt.

She didn't get much sleep that night at all, and when the rope was cut the next morning, she felt just as tired as she had the night before. Unfortunately, it wasn't a Sunday, so she had to go to work instead of thinking about everything she and Ida had talked about the night before.

The week went by without them seeing Luke at all. On Sunday, Ida moved in with Miss Charlotte Jones. Ellie went with her. Some people would think the flat was small and dreary with poor lighting and a tendency to be drafty on windy days, but Ida and Ellie were immediately charmed by the place and by Charlotte. The kindly middle-aged woman showed them Ida's new room, which held her own straw pallet and a small wardrobe to hold her belongings. Ida was barely able to hold back her excitement as she touched the straw mattress. "I can't believe I have my own bed! I'm livin' like a queen."

Charlotte chuckled from the doorway. "It ain't much. Just a straw pallet covered in some old linens. Yer young yet but give it time, and it'll make your back hurt."

"Not any worse than the two penny hangovers," Ida said. She grinned at Charlotte. "Thank you so much."

"No need to thank me, Missy. You're 'elpin' an old lady out with the rent and with the errands. I can't make it down to the market anymore, not in this weather. And my nephew is so busy at the bakery, I can hardly expect him to keep takin' care of me." The lady smiled at both of them. "Can I offer you ladies some tea?"

The three of them sat down at the table and drank hot tea, which was much more flavourful than the watered-down beverage they got from the market. After an hour of easy, friendly conversation between the three of them, Ellie knew it was time to go.

"It was lovely to meet you, Miss Charlotte," she said. "I cannot thank you enough for takin' Ida in. I know she'll be happy here."

"Of course, missy. And if there's ever a night when you can't get into the shelter, or you need a break from that blasted rope, then come here. I'm sure Ida won't mind sharin' her bed for the night."

"Of course not," said Ida. "But I don't think that will be a problem. Ellie's got 'erself a fella who is fixin' to marry her."

Charlotte's eyes twinkled. "Is that right?"

Ellie blushed. "Yes. Luke. I grew up with him. We both did. He repairs fishing equipment down by the wharf." He wasn't quite open for business yet. The last time they spoke, he had bought the small factory building, but he was busy fixing it up.

"Is he good to ye?"

"He's the best," Ellie said softly. In her peripheral vision, Ida beamed at her. "He's always been wonderful to me. He makes me feel safe and loved. Any girl would be lucky to 'ave 'im."

"Luke's in love with 'er," Ida said. "He spent years talkin' about giving her the life she deserves."

Ellie blushed harder, and Charlotte chuckled. "In my experience, a man like that is 'ard to find. My advice is to 'old onto 'im as tight as ye can."

Ellie bit her lip and nodded. "Yes," she said quietly. "I think I will."

After saying goodbye to Charlotte and hugging Ida goodbye, Ellie left the little flat and made her way down to the docks so she could see Luke. It felt strange walking to the docks without Ida, but she knew the younger woman needed some time to settle into her new place with Charlotte. She couldn't wait to tell Luke about their busy week.

When she reached the docks, Luke spotted her first in the crowd of people. "Ellie!" he said, running over to her. He grabbed her hands gently as soon as he could. "Where's Ida?"

"Oh Luke, the most wonderful thing happened." She told Luke about Charlotte and how she offered Ida a place to stay.

Luke looked amazed and happy. "And she's safe there? Did you go with her?"

Ellie nodded. "I 'elped her settle into her new bedroom– she has her own bedroom, isn't that marvellous? And I 'ad tea with her and Charlotte before I left. Miss Charlotte was so kind and wonderful. I know Ida is going to be so happy there."

Luke grinned. "Imagine that. Ida with her very own home." He grabbed her hand, looking suddenly nervous. "There's something I want to show ya."

"Okay." She was surprised. "Is it at your flat? We'll be late to supper if we don't go now."

"We're not having supper there tonight. I hope that's okay." He gestured to his satchel. "I packed some food for us, praying you'd come. And blankets."

"Where are we going?"

He took her hand in his. "I'll show you."

Luke led her through the crowded docks, to a lonely corner on one side of the wharf, where a single building stood by itself, a short distance away from the others.

Ellie stopped and stared at the building. She hardly recognized it. When she last saw it, the building looked like it was falling apart, with a dilapidated roof and its door off its hinges. The only thing going for it was a strong foundation.

Now, it looked completely different. The roof was repaired,

and the walls were reinforced with new lumber. A new door was in place as well. "How..."

"I've been really busy," he said. "For two weeks, I've been coming here after work and fixing it up, little by little. I got the building materials cheap because a shippin' company folded and left a warehouse full of lumber on the docks. It all got auctioned off for pennies on the dollar. With Sam and John's permission, I traded some fish in exchange for some buildin' expertise from some construction workers who hang out at the tavern near the docks. It's not the prettiest buildin', and there's still a lot of work to be done of course, but it will hold just as well as any other."

As Ellie stared at the building, Luke couldn't take his eyes off her. His usual confidence was gone. Instead, he looked nervous. "Do you want to go in?" he asked.

Ellie nodded. "Please."

Luke opened the door for her and led her inside. The building was divided into two stories. The ground story was completely empty. The floorboards were sturdy, and the windows let in some fading light from the sun, as well as light from the streetlamps.

"I'm going to get shutters for the windows," he said. "This part will be the shop. There ain't a lot of good fishin' equipment repair shops in these parts, so customers should come in quick enough."

"It's wonderful," Ellie said. "I know you will be able to find tons of fishermen lookin' for yer services."

He smiled. "I hope so. I hope I get enough so I can fix it up proper. I want this buildin' downright cozy and cheerful."

She smiled. "I'm sure you'll get there. You've already done an incredible job."

His smile grew, but he still looked hesitant. "Let me show ya the upstairs." He took her hand as they went to the narrow staircase on one side of the room. Up the stairs was a large room, with two windows and a small wood stove. It was almost completely empty.

"Don't worry. I've already jumped all over the floor to make sure it was stable. You'll be safe."

She followed him to the middle of the room and looked around. "What are you going to do with this part?"

"I'm turnin' it into a flat," he said softly.

Her eyes widened as she looked around. "Yer going to live here?"

"Yeah. It's better than the slums, ain't it? Besides, I own the buildin' so I can do what I want. I know it don't look like much now but picture some curtains on the windows. And a carpet on the floor. A table and some chairs, so we can eat properly. Maybe even a tablecloth on the table. Won't that be nice? The bed can go over there." He pointed to one side of the room. "And downstairs there's room for a wash basin and a clothin' line."

"Luke, I–"

"Wait. Don't say anythin' yet," he said. "I know yer nervous about marryin' me, and that's okay. I just wanted to show ya this place. I promised to give ya the life you deserve, and I think I can finally make good on the offer. I can give ya a home, Ellie. Even if ya decide ya don't want to marry me, you can stay in the flat, and I can keep livin' with John and Sam. It's all right."

She felt a lump in her throat as she looked around the flat– her new home. She couldn't believe Luke had done all of this for her. "Ya must have put in so much work."

"It was worth it," he whispered. "You're worth it, Ellie. It's okay if ya don't feel the same about me. Truly. But ya must know I'm in love with ya. I've always loved ya, and I will love ya until the day I die. Nothing will change that. I swear it."

Tears sprang to her eyes. "Are ya sure?" she asked. "Even after I couldn't save ya? Even after I couldn't save Daisy?"

His brow furrowed. "What do you mean ya couldn't save Daisy? I know ya tried your hardest. Ya did everything you could to save her, and I know that because ya did everything to save me when I got sick with fever."

"But ya told me to take care of the girls, and I failed." She was openly crying now. She didn't realize how long she had been holding this in, but she knew these tears were a long time coming. She didn't like crying much in front of Ida because she knew she had to be strong for her. But it was different with Luke. He always had enough strength for the both of them. He never judged her for crying, even when they barely knew each other.

It was still so easy to remember that night in the basement of the bakery, lying next to each other as Ida and Daisy slept.

"Cry all you want," he had whispered to her. "I won't 'old it against ya."

Now, in the present, Luke pulled her into his arms. "That's not yer fault," he said. "I know ya did everything ya could to save her." He rubbed her back gently to sooth her. "The truth is, I blame myself for her death too."

She looked up at him with a furrowed brow. "How could ya blame yourself? Ya weren't even 'ere."

"Exactly. I should have been. If I 'ad come back sooner somehow... or maybe fought off those thugs who took me away in the first place, then I could 'ave been here. I could 'ave stolen the medicine, or maybe even earned the money to buy it properly. I know it's not good to think these things. It doesn't solve nothin', and she wouldn't want us to feel guilty. But it's 'ard not to think of what if, you know?"

Ellie nodded and closed her eyes as she buried her face in his chest. Being in Luke's arms felt so good. She felt so safe with him, as if he really could protect her against the world, like he wanted to.

He kissed the top of her head, briefly. "Daisy would want us to 'ave a fresh start instead of making ourselves miserable for the rest of our lives. I know she don't blame ya any more than she blames me."

She knew he was right. And she wanted Luke so much. He was everything to her, and he knew she wouldn't love any other man the same way.

"Okay," she whispered. "I'll marry you."

He pulled back slightly to look at her. "Truly?"

"Yes." Nervousness and excitement filled her at the thought, and she gave him a delighted smile. "I love ya, Luke. I want to marry you."

He laughed and grabbed her waist. He picked her and twirled her around the room. "You've made me the 'appiest man in all of London, Ellie. I might even be the 'appiest man in the 'ole world."

She giggled. "I could say the same about myself."

He brushed her hair out of her face, gently. "I'm goin' to do right by ya, I swear it. We'll make this place nice and cozy, and once I'm earnin' enough coin, ya can quit sewing at the shop. Or if ya wish, you can keep workin'. Whatever ya want." He cupped her cheek with his hand, and she leaned into it, closing her eyes.

"You are so beautiful," he whispered. "And so kind."

"I can't believe ya want to marry me," Ellie whispered. "Ya can 'ave any girl you like. You're handsome and the kindest man I've ever known. I don't understand what ya see in me."

"'Ow can you say that?" He looked indignant at the thought. "You're beautiful and you're kind. You saved my life, and not just because ya nursed me back to 'ealth from that fever. It don't matter if I could find another girl or not. I want you. I've always wanted you. No one else." He rested his forehead against hers. "And if you don't mind, now that we're properly engaged, I would like to kiss ya. Would ya want that?"

She bit her lip, feeling a blush rise across her face as she nodded. "Please," she said. "I want to kiss ya, too."

Luke's fingers went to her chin, and he gently lifted her face to meet his own. He pressed his lips against hers, and they felt so warm and soft. Happiness soared through her, and her toes curled with excitement and joy.

He pulled back a moment later, looking just as happy and affected by the kiss. "Now, I don't know about ya, but I'm 'ungry. Let's eat."

He spread the blankets out on the wooden floor before pulling bread, meat, and cheese out of his satchel. Even though the blanket was ragged and thin, it cushioned them well enough as they sat down and ate their food while talking about everything and nothing. When they were finished, both had full bellies and were sleepy.

"I don't want to go to the two penny 'angover tonight," Ellie confessed. "Not by myself."

"You don't 'ave to," he whispered. "We can stay here, just like old times."

"But we ain't married yet," she said, blushing.

He chuckled. "I just want to sleep beside ye, Ellie. I like knowin' yer here next to me. I like knowin' yer safe and sound."

She smiled. "All right. That does sound nice. Besides, I always feel safe with you."

"Good," he murmured. "That's what I want."

They lay down on the blanket, keeping a little bit of space between them as they used their arms for pillows. For a moment, it felt like no time had passed at all, and they were just two street urchins, falling asleep together below an abandoned bakery. Ellie smiled, even as her heart felt like it was being squeezed. So much time had passed, and they had both changed so much. But they still loved each other all the same.

The two of them closed their eyes, and it wasn't long before Ellie fell asleep, listening to the quiet, even sounds of Luke breathing.

CHAPTER 11

It was an unusually warm day in February. The sun was shining in the sky, and the snow was melting in the streets, creating small rivers of water, running into the gutters. Luke swore he could even hear the birds singing.

It was a perfect day for a wedding.

He woke up that morning in his new flat. He had been busy getting it nice and comfortable, ever since Ellie agreed to marry him. Now there was a proper straw pallet for them, and a table and chairs for dinner. They even had an extra couple of chairs for company and some proper dishes. Curtains decorated the windows as well, to give it a nice cozy feeling.

All the furniture was modest. The curtains, purchased from the rag seller, were tattered and fraying at the edges, and the table and chairs were rickety and prone to splintering. He didn't have the tablecloth yet, and he didn't have a proper rug on the floor, which was much too cold in the dead of winter, but the flat felt like a proper home.

He felt a rush of pride, knowing he would take Ellie back here tonight, where they could have a nice supper together, and they could sleep in a real bed. He knew she hadn't slept in a real bed since her parents died, all those years ago, and he was happy he was able to provide her with one again. He was also proud that he was able to make a home for himself as well. Who would have thought a street vagrant like him would be able to make a decent living for himself and a family? It was a dream come true for himself.

He got dressed in his nicest clothes. It was only a tattered white shirt and black pants along with his work boots, but at least everything was clean and didn't smell like fish. That was an improvement at least.

When he finished getting dressed, he heard a knock at the door downstairs.

"Closed for business!" he shouted. "Come back tomorrow!"

With some help from Sam and John, word had spread about a decent repairman for fishing gear who charged reasonable prices. He now had a steady supply of customers that allowed him to make a decent living.

"It's us," John shouted from outside. "Come on, man, you don't wanna keep a bride waitin' on her weddin' day!"

Luke ran down the stairs and opened the front door to see his two best friends. He grinned and wrapped both into a hug.

Sam laughed and clapped him on the back as John extracted himself from the hug, grumbling even though his eyes were twinkling.

"Someone's in a good mood," the younger brother said. "Ye'd think ye were gettin' hitched or somethin'."

"It still feels like a dream," Luke confessed. "'Ow in the world did I get a girl like 'er?"

"Charm and good looks," Sam said. "I should know. I charmed many a girl back in my day."

"Ye couldn't have charmed a barnacle off a rock," John shot back.

Sam made an offended sound while Luke laughed. He was happy the brothers were willing and able to take a day off for his wedding. The two of them were always working, so Luke hardly saw them much anymore, but he still considered them his best friends.

The three of them walked to the small church, where he was going to marry. They went inside the small church, which was a single room with hard, uncomfortable pews and a small podium where the vicar preached. The man was up there now, reading his Bible and probably preparing for his sermon later that day.

Father Bishop shut the book and smiled at the men as they came in. "You must be here for the wedding," he said. "Which one of you is Luke?"

"That's me," Luke said, shaking the man's hand. "Where are the girls? Are they here yet?"

He couldn't stop the feeling of trepidation. If something happened to them on the way here... No, he couldn't think like that. Sometimes his impulse to constantly worry over Ellie and Ida would get to be too much, and he needed to tell himself to stop.

"They aren't here yet," said the vicar. "But I'm sure they will arrive soon."

Just then, the door opened, and Ida came in, along with Miss Charlotte, and a young lady he knew to be Amelia. He had only met Charlotte and Amelia a couple of times before, but he enjoyed their company very much.

Ida grinned up at him. "She's coming. She just needs a moment."

Luke nodded, not trusting himself to speak. He hoped she wasn't changing her mind.

Charlotte's eyes twinkled as she looked at him. "I've been to enough weddings to know it's common for the bride to get nervous and need a moment to right 'erself. Don't worry. She ain't backing out."

Luke stood at the altar with Sam and John on one side of him, and on the other was Ida, Charlotte and Amelia. He stared at the door, willing for it to open. When the door finally did open, its hinges squeaking, his heart leaped into his throat.

Ellie stood in the doorway, looking even more breathtaking than he had ever seen her. Her blue dress was freshly laundered, and she had new boots on her feet. Her hair was done up in a braided bun and decorated with a light blue ribbon she borrowed from Amelia. She carried a bouquet of dried flowers as she stepped into the church. She gave Luke a nervous smile.

He had never seen a more beautiful woman in his life. Not even in his wildest dreams did he imagine Ellie would look so pretty while on her way to marry him. He couldn't take his eyes off her as she joined him at the altar.

The vicar smiled and began the service. But Luke barely heard him. All he could do was look at Ellie and marvel about how he must be the luckiest man in the world.

Ellie watched him with a shy smile on her face and a blush on her cheeks.

Luke straightened, realizing they were saying the wedding vows. The vicar turned to him. "Luke, do you take this woman to be your wife, to love and cherish, until death do you part?"

"I do," he murmured. It was the easiest vow he had ever made because he had always known he would love and cherish her until the day he died, whether she decided to be his bride or not.

"I do," Ellie said quietly when it was her turn.

The man smiled and looked at Luke. "You may kiss the bride."

Luke pulled her in for a kiss while everyone cheered. They broke apart, grinning, but Luke held onto her hand. He didn't think he would ever be able to let go.

Both smiled and laughed, and a calmness settled over Luke as he gazed at his wife. They would be all right. Whatever hardships they faced now would be a million times easier than everything they faced in the past because they had each other and all their wonderful friends. They would be safe and comfortable in their new home. No more begging for coins. No more starving. Everything was going to be okay.

"I love you," he whispered to her.

She gazed up at him, the love and affection clear on her face. "I love you too."

CHAPTER 12

IT WAS A HOT JUNE MORNING, but the breeze from the ocean cooled Ellie down as she hung up clothing to dry on the clothesline behind Luke's shop. After getting married, she gave up her job at the dress shop. It would take too long to get there from her new home on the wharf, and she didn't need to work there anyway. She could stay home and take in laundry for even more money than she made sewing, and with less work involved. Not that it was really needed. Luke managed to provide both with a comfortable life from his job of repairing fishing equipment.

But they would need some extra money soon. She was sure of that. Ellie touched her belly briefly, feeling a flutter of fear and excitement, just like she felt when she agreed to marry Luke. She was going to be a mother.

She had known for a little over a month, but she hadn't told Luke yet. She couldn't find the right time to do so yet. She wanted it to be perfect.

After she finished hanging out the clothing to dry, she hurried inside. Luke was busy at work, repairing a fishing net, but he stopped his work to pull her into his arms and give her a kiss.

"You look more beautiful every day, my love," he whispered in her ear.

She giggled. "You always say that."

"And it's always true." He kissed the tip of her nose which made her smile.

"I 'ave to go prepare supper," she said, stepping back.

He nodded. "I'll be up soon. I'm almost done with my work for tonight." He smiled down at her. "I love ya," he whispered.

She grinned up at him. "I love ya, too."

As he got busy with the net again, she went upstairs. She was going to tell him tonight and she wanted everything to be perfect.

She changed into her only other dress, which was freshly cleaned. She also knew it was Luke's favorite dress on her. He said it was because it complemented her eyes, but she knew it was because it was the dress she was wearing when she married him.

After changing, she started to make supper. She had cooked a bit of roast meat and vegetables over the woodstove earlier in the day, and now she put the food on the plates, along with a piece of bread each. It wasn't long ago that she would have considered a meal like this as a feast fit to split between four people, and now it was something she ate regularly. Even though she would never forget how it felt to be starving on the streets, she knew she wouldn't experience that again, and not for the first time, she counted her blessings.

She poured them both a cup of tea before she undid her hair from its messy braid. As carefully as she could, she twisted it into a neat bun. She had just finished fastening it into place when she heard footsteps on the stairs. She turned around with a smile.

Luke looked at her with a sharp eye. "You look pretty," he said. "Is there a special occasion?" He took a step closer and grabbed her hands. "I know it's not yer birthday, nor mine. And it's much too soon to be our anniversary."

She smiled at him, feeling nervous, but also excited. "You're right. It's a special occasion. But let's eat first. I don't want the food to get cold."

He chuckled. "That ain't likely to happen in this heat." But he sat down anyway

The two of them ate in silence, only occasionally glancing at each other during the meal. The curiosity was plain on Luke's face, but he restrained himself from asking again until the last bite was eaten.

"I've been wrackin' my mind, but for the life of me I can't tell why today is a special occasion." He chuckled awkwardly. "Can ya just tell me?"

She swallowed and took a deep breath. "I am with child."

He froze for a moment before his eyes widened. "Truly?" He breathed out the word.

She nodded. "I've been thinkin' it for a little over a month. I am sure now."

Luke laughed, a look of sheer joy lighting his face. "This is the best news I have heard all day."

He stood up and pulled her into his arms and twirled her around. "We're goin' to be parents, ain't we? You will be a wonderful mum."

He leaned down to kiss her. His kiss was full of love, but it was also a silent promise to take care of her and protect her. It was the same promise he made every time he kissed her, but Ellie knew the promise was now also for their child she carried in her womb.

"You'll be a wonderful da," she said, smiling up at him. "I can just see a wee little one, following ya around the shop, asking a million questions."

He grinned. "Imagine that," he whispered. "I never thought I would be a da. Not really."

"You must have known it was a possibility when you married me," Ellie said, laughing.

He cupped her face with his hands. His touch was gentle and warm, and she couldn't help but close her eyes with contentment from the feeling.

"I know," he murmured. "But truth be told, for most of my life I didn't even think I was worthy of marryin' ya. I thought my luck would run out eventually. But not only are ya my wife, but you're also carryin' my child. I doubt I'll ever stop bein' amazed at how lucky I am."

He placed a hand on her stomach. It was still flat, but in a few months, he would be able to feel a baby kicking in there.

"I'm the lucky one," Ellie said. "I still don't know how I found a man as kind and wonderful as you, not to mention got ya to marry me."

"Who wouldn't want to marry a lady a perfect as you?" he murmured. "There are probably princes out there who would kneel at your feet for the chance of marryin' ya. And yet somehow, ya chose me anyway."

Ellie smiled at the fantastical thought. Even if princes were lining up for her hand in marriage, she would choose Luke every time. He owned her heart completely, just as she owned his. And soon they were going to be parents.

They embraced in the middle of their cozy little flat as the sun set over the water, casting the room in a warm, orange glow. Peace and contentment filled Ellie, like it always did when Luke held her in his arms like this. It was a reminder that everything was going to be okay. Somehow, against all odds, the two of them had found their happy ending, and she would count her lucky stars every night for this new, wonderful life with Luke.

The End

CONTINUE READING...

T HANK you for reading **The Orphan's Oath! Are you wondering what to read next?** Why not read **The Shoemaker? Here's a sneak peek for you:**

London, 1840

Eight-year-old Eliza Harris carried the heavy bucket of water from the street water pipe to their one-room tenement and placed it on the floor. A little of it had splashed out on her short journey back, and she was thankful they lived on the ground floor. She would never be able to take that heavy bucket up those treacherous stairs that looked like they would crumble any minute.

Outside the thin door, children wailed, adults shouted, and dogs howled, filling the air of her run-down dwelling. It was an everyday occurrence, and Eliza didn't take notice of it anymore. Her thin arms ached, but she only sighed and carried on with her routine chores as she did every day.

The cold snap had set in for it was now October. Biting wind blew in from the cracks of the walls of the one-room tenement she, her two younger sisters, and her father stayed in. She wished for warmth and envied those who could afford to have a fireplace with a lovely fire blazing in their front rooms. Sometimes on dark days, she would walk along the grander streets, and when no one was looking, she would strain to peer into the houses. She'd imagine the warmth of the fire on her face, and she would stay there for a few moments, yearning.

One such day, she wasn't so lucky and had to flee when a peeler saw her; he clearly thought she was up to no good because she was ragged. She ran as fast as her small legs could carry her as he chased her with a baton. She'd not been back to that street since. But one day, she vowed to work in one of those houses, if only to be warm and comfortable, and then she could look after her two sisters properly, give them nourishing food and decent clothes to wear.

Wrapping her dead mother's tatty shawl around her thin shoulders, Eliza went to check on her sisters, Annie, who was six, and Dora, who was two. Annie stayed with Dora while Eliza went to fetch the water. The girls were huddled together under the two thin blankets Eliza had managed to buy from a rag man.

"I'm hungry," moaned Annie, her deep blue eyes hollow and miserable.

"I know, Annie. I'll see if we 'ave some bread. Dora, da ya want some, too?"

Dora looked up at Eliza with her big brown eyes and nodded. She didn't look completely well, which worried Eliza. She'd been slow these past few days and seemed limp, and a bit hot to the touch.

Click Here to Continue Reading!

https://www.ticahousepublishing.com/victorian-romance.html

THANKS FOR READING

If you love Victorian Romance, **Click Here**

https://victorian.subscribemenow.com/

to hear about all **New Faye Godwin Romance Releases! I will let you know as soon as they become available!**

Thank you, Friends! If you enjoyed *The Orphan's Oath,* would you kindly take a couple minutes to leave a positive review on Amazon? It only takes a moment, and positive reviews truly make a difference. Thank you so much! I appreciate it!

Much love,

Faye Godwin

MORE FAYE GODWIN VICTORIAN ROMANCES!

We love rich, dramatic Victorian Romances and have a library of Faye Godwin titles just for you! (Remember that ALL of Faye's Victorian titles can be downloaded FREE with Kindle Unlimited!)

CLICK HERE to discover Faye's Complete Collection of Victorian Romance!

https://ticahousepublishing.com/victorian-romance.html

ABOUT THE AUTHOR

Faye Godwin has been fascinated with Victorian Romance since she was a teen. After reading every Victorian Romance in her public library, she decided to start writing them herself —which she's been doing ever since. Faye lives with her husband and young son in England. She loves to travel throughout her country, dreaming up new plots for her romances. She's delighted to join the Tica House Publishing family and looks forward to getting to know her readers.

contact@ticahousepublishing.com

Printed in Dunstable, United Kingdom